WILD SKY

Praise for *Wild Sky*, The Relic Hunters #2

"Non-stop adventure with an exciting blend of magic and dystopia. Sinister villains, strange magic and thrilling adventure. I loved it!"

Claire Fayers, author of
The Accidental Pirates series,
Mirror Magic and *Storm Hound*

"Raging seas, snowy lands, fortresses and monasteries – the quest for the relics continues at an exhilarating pace. You won't put it down!"

Jude Lennon, author of
the *Hal* series and other books

Praise for *Eternal Seas*, The Relic Hunters #1

"This action-packed blend of magical fantasy with classic kids' adventuring is a swashbuckling read for 8+ year-olds, peppered with soft line-drawings and propelled by a strong sense of urgency."

LoveReading4Kids

"A thrilling and magical adventure with plenty of hair-raising chases and a villain readers will love to hate. ETERNAL SEAS is a must-read for young fantasy fans."

Madeline Dyer, author of the *Untamed* series

"ETERNAL SEAS is a compelling adventure that weaves mystery and intrigue into a tantalising plot for the reader to enjoy. The writing has a lyrical quality and almost seems to capture the movement of the sea as the story unfolds. A very enjoyable read."

Jude Lennon, author of *Hal and the End Street,* the *Lamby* series and other children's books

"An exciting debut novel by Lexi Rees that takes us on a roller coaster adventure ride over high seas to mysterious places and brims with magic and intrigue. Young readers will love this book."

Shalbey Bellaman, author of *Dragons in the Looking Glass* and *Jack in the Wallows*

ALSO BY THE AUTHOR

Eternal Seas

Creative Writing Skills

WILD SKY

LEXI REES

Matador
9 Priory Business Park,
Wistow Road, Kibworth Beauchamp,
Leicestershire. LE8 0RX
Tel: 0116 279 2299
Email: books@troubador.co.uk
Web: www.troubador.co.uk/matador
Twitter: @matadorbooks

ISBN 978 1838591 939

British Library Cataloguing in Publication Data.
A catalogue record for this book is available from the British Library.

Printed and bound by CPI Group (UK) Ltd, Croydon, CR0 4YY
Typeset in 12pt Aldine401 BT by Troubador Publishing Ltd, Leicester, UK

Matador is an imprint of Troubador Publishing Ltd

For Finlay,
always my inspiration.

Algol,

Do not be misled into thinking they have won. Finding the first relic and freeing the Sea-Tamer magic is nothing compared to what we can and will accomplish. We will destroy the other relics and their magic. The clans shall not rise to challenge us.

The Relic Hunters are weak. The girl lacks her full powers, and the boy has proven himself to be headstrong with a foolish attachment to Morgan. We can turn these weaknesses to our advantage.

Without a shadow of doubt, the other blood magic children are lost to this world. They do not concern me. As for the escape of Pippin, I assure you, she is nothing more than a silly child.

As promised, I have a gift for you. Something beyond your wildest dreams. Something no human has ever offered you. I will not spoil the surprise by telling you now, but you will not be disappointed.

Together, we will rule this world, and the world beyond.

Your loyal servant,

Sir Waldred

Lord of all Earth-Wanderers

ONE

PROPHECY

Only a shimmer remains of his body. With every word, the elder's voice fades further, 'Morgan also seeks the relics, but not for the clans. She will give them to Sir Waldred. You *must* find the relics before her or the clan magic will be lost forever, and all our sacrifices will have been for nothing.' Then, with a flicker of silver light, he's gone.

The fireplace lies cold and empty. Faded tapestries hang limply from the cold, grey, stone walls. A dark wooden table fills the middle of the Great Hall, the polish giving it a soft sheen despite the gloom. Pulled in tight around the table are twelve, tall wooden chairs. Brown leather seats, brittle and cracked with age, sag in the middle, yet no trace of their recent occupants remains. The clan elders are gone. We're alone. Our breathing echoes in the emptiness.

I shiver.

My sister, Aria, slips the hyrshu Air-Rider charm, a gift from one of the elders which marks her as a blood-magic child, over her head and tucks it under her shirt. My hand automatically goes to the pirffu Sea-Tamer charm on its leather cord around my neck.

'We have to find the Air-Rider relic before Morgan,' I say.

'But I don't know where to start looking. They didn't give us any directions,' Aria says, clenching her fists.

'The journal?' I suggest. 'What's in it? Maybe there's a clue.'

Aria opens it, her brows knit in concentration. 'There's a riddle on the last page.'

'What does it say?'

She reads aloud.

Where white eagles soar and no man can walk,
Above the clouds, yet still on the ground,
Lies the secret of which Air-People talk.
The winged girl must raise her clan around,
When the moon is cold and the stars point true,
For the time has come to start our world anew.

'Well that's not much of a clue is it,' I say with a scowl. I shove my hands into my pockets.

'I think I understand it,' Aria says. 'Or at least some of it. The Cold Moon is the last full moon of the year, and it's soon.'

'And?'

'That night, we need to look at the stars. There must be some kind of sign in the sky. We'll need a telescope though. The bigger the better. Can we get to an observatory before then?'

'There's the Royal Observatory in Greenwich, but I don't like the idea of going back to New London,' Dad says.

We all shake our heads. Last time we were in New London, we only just escaped with our lives.

'I know where we can go,' Pippin says. 'Spitbank Fort. It's an old army stronghold. Officially, it's been empty since the Second World War, although unofficially ...' Her voice trails off and her eyes sink to the floor.

'Unofficially?' Aria prompts her to continue.

Pippin raises her eyes. 'Unofficially, Sir Waldred used it as a secret research base. But it's empty now. He abandoned it years ago. It should be safe ... I think.' Her eyes glaze over. She might be younger than me, but her eyes tell a different story. Who knows what horrors she witnessed during her time with Sir Waldred. She blinks and carries on, 'We won't be seen, and there's a massive telescope.'

'Sounds like a possibility then. Where is it though? I've not heard of it,' Dad says.

'It's not big so I'm not surprised you've not heard of it. It's in the middle of the sea off the south coast of England—'

'Why would Sir Waldred set up a base there? He hates the sea,' I interrupt.

'I know. He was in a really bad mood the whole time. Even badder tempered than usual. It was funny when we were on the boat going there though, he got really seasick. And then there was the time when I put seaweed in his spaghetti, and he was sick for a week and ...'

Aria snorts. 'Seaweed? Yuck.'

Mum stops her. 'Pippin, you can tell us the stories later, but we need to know why he was there?'

'Right. Yes. Of course. For the light, I guess. No. For the dark,' Pippin says.

Confused, I screw my face up.

'Light pollution,' Pippin continues. 'You need to be away from the city lights to use a telescope properly. Sir Waldred couldn't do that in New London. Spitbank Fort was perfect.'

'But what was he doing there? Why did he need a telescope? Do you think he knew about the clue in the stars?' Aria fires questions at Pippin.

Pippin scratches her head. 'Uhm, I don't know. He dragged all his scientists over there last year, set up the observatory, and locked himself away in it. He even slept in there. Never said exactly what he was doing, but he studied the sky the whole time we were there. Every. Single. Day. It was so boring. I don't think he found any clues though, he was too grumpy.'

'Whew, maybe we still have a head start on him.' Aria breathes a sigh of relief.

Mum shakes her head. 'Not much of a head start. We're miles away and Morgan could be anywhere. We'd better get going.'

'Mum's right. Let's get back to the boat,' Dad says, turning to leave. He glances around the empty room. 'Nothing left to do here.'

On the way out, Aria pauses by one of the chairs. Just a few minutes earlier, one of the Air-Rider elders had been sitting there. Tears glisten in Aria's eyes as her fingers trace the intricate wooden carving on the seat-back. I want to ask if she can see more than I can, if there's any trace of life within it, but I bite my tongue. It's not the right time. Instead, I wrap my arm around her and nudge her towards the door, her eyes still fixed on the carving.

Unseen forces raise the heavy iron portcullis and we emerge, blinking, from the gloomy hall into daylight. The instant we pass through the gate, the portcullis crashes down behind us. Castle Gylen has barricaded itself again.

My back pressed against the castle wall, I scan the landscape for Sir Waldred. After our battle a few hours ago, the ground swallowed him up. I'm not foolish enough to think we defeated him. He's lurking somewhere. Watching. Waiting. I shudder.

'Do you think Sir Waldred is out there?' Aria asks.

'Yes. He won't let us out of his sight. Not now the race to the next relic is on.'

In a silent, straggly line, we trudge down the steep path to the rocky beach. Our boat, *The Alcina*, is still anchored in the bay. I breathe a sigh of relief. The sea churns restlessly and the boat strains against the anchor, drifting round so it's beam-on to us. 'Oh,' I say, clapping my hand to my mouth.

'What do you mean, "oh"?' Mum asks.

My hand shakes as I point. 'Sir Waldred has been on our boat. Look, he's hoisted an Earth-Wanderer flag.'

Dad's face is a mask of fury. 'How dare he,' he spits. 'He'd better not have damaged anything, or found ...' He clamps his mouth shut and stomps across the beach. 'Hurry up,' he snaps.

I rush over and help him drag the dinghy, a little wooden rowing boat, across the stony beach down towards the sea. 'Found what? Have we got anything on the boat that Sir Waldred might be after, now the Sea-Tamer relic has been delivered?'

'Nothing in particular,' he mutters.

Icy water bites my ankles as I wade out. Knee-deep in the water, Dad holds the dinghy steady while we clamber in. 'Aren't your feet freezing, Dad?' I ask, wriggling my toes to bring them back to life.

'No. It's my Scottish blood.' He forces a laugh and rolls his sleeves up as if it was mid-summer. The dinghy wobbles as he climbs in. Aria and I pick up an oar each and start to row briskly and rhythmically through the waves, cutting a path back to our floating home.

We pull up alongside *The Alcina*. In stories, people "leap nimbly aboard". That's not true. The sea never stops moving, even on a calm day. One by one, we stand on the side of the dinghy, while *The Alcina* jerks about in the waves, then we "grab and scramble".

'Whoops,' Pippin giggles as she slips on the edge and tumbles back almost capsizing us.

Once we're all aboard, Dad storms over to the mast and yanks Sir Waldred's flag down. Face like thunder, he screws it up into a ball and flings it overboard. A gust of wind catches the flag, and it lands on the water, spread out like a tablecloth. It floats for a few seconds before the sea swallows it. Once it's sunk out of sight, we methodically check every inch of the boat.

'Anyone find any damage?' Dad asks.

'None as far as I can see,' Aria says, hesitantly.

'Just because we can't see any damage, doesn't mean he didn't do something,' Dad says. Under his breath, I catch him muttering, 'We should have left someone on guard.' He turns away and buries his head in his hands.

Mum pats him on the back. 'You weren't to know he would dare to come on board. Anyway, there's nothing we can do about it now. Let's get going. Everyone, keep your eyes open.'

As I walk away, Dad whispers something in Mum's ear. I strain to hear. 'I think he took it. What are we going to do?' He slaps his hand on his forehead. 'It's a disaster.'

'Don't worry, Ragnar,' Mum says. She smiles, but her face is grim. 'I'm sure they'll turn up. Probably just buried in the mess. It's about time we had a bit of a tidy up.'

'What did he take?' I ask.

Startled, Dad turns around. 'Finn, I thought you'd gone,' he says. 'Nothing to worry about. I just can't find some papers, but Mum's right, they'll be here somewhere.'

A heavy silence hangs over us as we prepare for the voyage. Aria winches the rowing boat up onto the deck and lashes it down for the journey. The motor on the windlass whines as it picks up the heavy anchor chain. The anchor grinds over the bow roller and clanks into its holder. I secure it in place with a thick steel pin. As soon as we're free, the sea forces us away from the island. This place really does not like visitors. Dad's right, there's no point hanging around. I'm ready to escape from this bitter, unwelcoming, shore.

Dad turns the boat into the wind to raise the main sail then sets a southerly course.

I glance back at the castle, perched high on the jagged rocks with the steel-grey sea crashing below it. Something catches my attention. I screw my eyes up and peer at the island. Something looks different. A little less bleak? A spot of green amongst the barren rocks? I pick up my binoculars and turn the dials to focus on the speck of colour, but we're too far away now. Probably imagined it anyway. With a shrug, I turn my back on the island.

TWO

HIDE

'Finn, can you cast a protective mist to cloak us from Sir Waldred?' Mum asks. 'I don't want him, or his trackers, to spot us.'

My stomach twists into a tight knot at the mention of the trackers. That's the last thing we need. We've escaped them twice before. Twice more than anybody else. Our luck can't hold. I close my eyes and stretch my arms out wide, palms facing down. My fingertips tingle as the blood-magic rushes through my veins. The pirffu charm around my neck begins to throb, ba-dum ba-dum ba-dum, keeping time with my own heartbeat. Despite the cold Scottish air, a bead of sweat trickles down my back. Slowly, I raise my arms above my head. My heart thumps so hard against my ribcage it hurts, and the pirffu charm pounds out its drumbeat, ba-dum ba-dum ba-dum. I pause for a minute. When

I open my eyes, the island has vanished. Everything has vanished. The boat. My family. Disorientated, I spin round.

'Maybe just a bit too much mist, Finn.' Mum's voice drifts through the murk. 'That's a real pea-souper you've created. None of us have X-ray vision. In this, it'll be five minutes before one of us trips and falls overboard.'

I hang my head. 'Sorry, Mum, I know my magic is a bit unpredictable. Promise I'll return for proper training after Aria finds the Air-Rider relic.' With a sigh, I drag the fog back down into the sea.

'Not to worry. Take a few deep breaths, then try again,' Mum advises. She starts to count aloud for me, 'In for one. And out for two. In for three ...'

I force the image of the trackers out of my mind. Arms outstretched, my eyes squeezed tight shut, I try again.

Eyes still closed, I hear Mum's voice. 'Much better, a nice light mist. Just enough to cover us, and we won't be bumping into things on the boat. You can always make it thicker if we spot any trouble.'

At the mention of trouble, the image of trackers burns its way into the back of my eyeballs again. I rub my eyes and blink it away.

'How long will the trip to Spitbank Fort take us?' Aria asks.

Dad frowns. 'Must be a good six hundred miles down the coast from here. I'll check the exact distance on the charts, but it should take about ten days, give or take.'

'When's the Cold Moon? Can we get there in time?' I ask, glancing at our boat: old, solid, heavy. *The Alcina* has kept us safe through many adventures, but she's no jet-ship. Her thick wooden hull wasn't built for speed; at best, we can do six, maybe seven, knots.

Aria gazes at the sky. 'Next Monday.'

I count the days off on my fingers. 'That's cutting it fine. We'll only arrive on Sunday.'

Dad sniffs the air and shakes his head. 'Wind's against us. Better plan for two weeks.'

'No! That's too late. We'll miss the Cold Moon,' Aria says, her eyes flaring. 'We can't miss it. The prophecy specifically says the Cold Moon; the last full moon of the year. That date must be really important. If we miss it, we'll have to wait another year before we can solve the clue. What if Sir Waldred or Morgan find the relic before then? They'll destroy it and the clan magic will be lost forever. No. We'll have to sail all day, and all night ...' Her voice falters.

Last time we did a night sail, we got caught in a huge storm. My fists clench automatically, as if I'm still gripping onto the wheel, battling to keep us from capsizing and being dragged down into the depths of the sea. I recall Dad lying unconscious on the deck after an accident. My fault ...

'It wasn't your fault, Finn, I should have been paying attention,' Dad says, apparently reading my mind. 'Aria's right though. We'd better not miss the Cold Moon. If we don't anchor overnight, that'll buy us several days' leeway. Are you OK to do night shifts? I can't do it on my own, this needs to be a team effort.'

Through gritted teeth, I hear my voice say, 'Night shifts are fine.' I force myself to unclench my fists.

'Yippee,' Pippin says, grinning from ear to ear. 'Sounds fun. I've always wanted to do a night sail.'

Everyone grimaces.

'Why are you all pulling faces at me?' Pippin asks. She's still bouncing with excitement, the only one of us who sees this as a big adventure. Of course, she wasn't with us during the big storm.

'Night sails aren't fun,' Aria says, her voice flat and strained. 'They're hard work, and scary. You can't see what's out there, and it's so creepy and quiet.'

Hands on her hips, Pippin juts her chin forward. 'I'm not scared of the dark.' She's only nine, one year younger than Aria, and three years younger than me. There's no need to scare her, so I let it slide.

Mum takes Aria's hand and gives it a squeeze. 'It'll be fine this time,' she whispers. 'We're not going to be miles offshore. We're just running down the coast. If there's any bad weather forecast, we'll duck into a harbour. Promise.'

I open my mouth to point out that we don't have time to stop, that we *must* keep going in order to arrive before the Cold Moon, but I catch Mum glaring at me and shut it.

'OK,' Aria says, squaring her shoulders, her jaw set firm. 'We have to. We don't have a choice. I won't fail the Air-Riders.'

'We won't let you fail,' I say.

Mum smiles and nods. Dad claps Aria on the back. Pippin leaps up and flings her arms around her.

'That's decided then,' Dad says. 'I'm so proud of you all.'

With Dad at the helm and the sails set, there's nothing to do on deck. A loud rumble from my stomach reminds me we haven't eaten all day. I head to the galley, the tiny boat kitchen, to prepare supper; serving up bowls of thick beef stew and steaming mugs of sweet tea. They vanish in a flash. Clearly, I wasn't the only one whose tummy was grumbling.

'Delish, Finn,' Aria says.

'Yummy. Can we have noodles tomorrow?' Pippin chirps. 'I love noodles.'

'You can cook if you're going to be fussy,' I say.

'Done. I'm a brilliant cook, you know,' Pippin says. 'Chicken noodles it is. I think I'll do a nice ginger sauce. Slightly spicy maybe. Do we have chopsticks?'

With a worried look on her face, Mum nods.

Pippin skips round the table. 'This will be the best meal you've ever had.'

The winds are kind, blowing a comfortable force four south-westerly and we make swift progress down the coast. As we travel further south, the sea turns from steel-grey to denim-blue. Every couple of hours we need to tack so our course is a zigzag, but at least it's a quick, easy zigzag, not a hard, bumpy slog into the wind. After each tack, I check the tell-tales, strands of thread that fly from the sails, and use them to help me adjust the angle of the sails to get the best speed. We take turns on deck, snatching a few hours' sleep in between our shifts. We're permanently tired.

Through the mist, a hazy outline of land on our left provides some variation to the scenery as it rises and falls from cliffs into bays. Days blend into each other with the monotony of a long voyage. I stretch out on my bunk but can't seem to drop off to sleep. I give up and get up, pacing round the boat restlessly, looking for something to do. Drawn by the heady aromas arising from the galley, I find Pippin surrounded by an assortment of pots and pans and a mountain of vegetable peelings. My mouth waters as I reach forward to steal a taste. 'Where did you learn to cook like this?'

'Oh, here and there. You know how it is.'

'Not really. I can just about manage not to burn toast, but this is something else, like professional chef stuff. Who taught—'

'I guess I just picked it up along the way.' She turns her back on me and starts chopping vegetables at lightning speed.

'But—'

'I don't want to talk about it,' she snaps.

I frown. I know she had a difficult time with Sir Waldred before she joined us, so I don't want to push her, but there seems to be much more to her past than she's told us about. I wander off to find Aria. Curled into a ball in her favourite corner on deck, Aria's buried in a heavy-looking book. I squeeze in beside her and draw my knees up to my chin.

'What are you reading?' I ask.

She puts the book down. 'Astronomy. Thought I should do some research before the Cold Moon.' She peers into the midday gloom. 'Look, the sun's trying to burn through. Could we drop the mist for a few hours? I'd love to feel the sun on my skin.'

'Sorry. We can't risk the trackers finding us,' I say.

She sighs, tugging the hood on her bright yellow waterproof jacket forward so it falls further over her face, 'I know, but it would be nice. Everything in my room is soggy.'

'Mine too, but it's too dangerous.' I catch a glimpse of her face, half-hidden under the hood. Her eyes are red and puffy. 'Have you been crying? What's wrong?'

'Nothing.'

'Doesn't look like nothing. You can tell me.'

'I'm worried,' Aria says, wiping her nose with the back of her hand.

'About what?'

'I'm worried that I don't know what to look for when we get to the observatory. What if I miss the clue?'

THREE

SEEK

'Don't be silly, Aria. You'll work it out. Plus, we're all here to help. Perhaps there are more clues in the journal?' Despite us all practically begging her, Aria hasn't let anyone else read it. In fact, I don't think it's been out of her sight since the clan elder gave it to her. She probably sleeps with it beneath her pillow. I try a blatant hint. 'We could go through it together, if you like?'

With a nod, Aria stands up and heads below decks, pausing to hang her raincoat up in the locker. Surprised she's finally agreed to let me see the journal, it takes me a moment to gather my thoughts before I spring into action. I fly down the stairs after her, shrugging off my coat and tossing it into a corner.

Aria pauses on her way past the galley. 'Are you finished, Pippin?'

'Nearly.'

'Hurry up then,' Aria says. 'We've got something to do.'

Pippin sweeps the prepared vegetables into a bowl and skips after Aria.

While my cabin's tucked tight into the bow, shaped like a triangle to fit the space, Aria and Pippin share a long, narrow cabin which runs down one side of the boat. Their beds are lined up end to end along the wall, so when they lie down, their toes nearly meet in the middle. Above the beds is a brightly coloured mural of painted birds. It brings a pop of colour into the clean, white room.

Aria sits crossed legged in the middle of the floor and gestures for to us to join her. 'Shoes off,' she squeals. My foot hovers mid-air. I kick off the only very slightly grubby boots and walk, barefoot, across the white painted floorboards.

Sporting a pair of mismatched socks with holes in the toes, Pippin skates across the smooth, wooden floor and plonks herself down beside Aria. Once we're settled in a circle, Aria places the journal in the middle. 'You both need to read this—'

'Already read it,' Pippin announces.

Aria frowns. 'You read it? How? When?'

'While you were asleep. You must have bumped it during the night. It fell on the floor so I thought I should pick it up for you and then I wasn't sleepy so …' Pippin looks at us, 'Oops. Did I do the wrong thing?'

'Yes! You shouldn't read someone's diary without asking them first,' Aria says, her voice sharper than usual.

'But it's not your diary. I mean, it's yours, but you didn't write it. So, I didn't think the diary rule applied. You don't mind, do you?' Pippin looks genuinely concerned.

Aria's face softens and she smiles at her. 'You're right. It's just a diary, not my diary. It's fine.'

Pippin beams at her, then pulls one sock off, tossing it into the corner of the room, where it lies, accusing us with its messiness.

Aria ignores the sock-mess and takes a deep breath. 'I'm sure there are more clues in here. Lots of it is scribbled out, but we could start with the riddle.' Aria flicks to the end of the journal and reads the first line of the riddle aloud …

Where white eagles soar and no man can walk,

Pippin interrupts again, 'That's the line I keep thinking about too.'

'How many times did you read it?' Aria asks.

'Just once. Maybe twice. Actually, it was probably three times. There was a lot to think about. Anyway, that's not the point. Remember how the elder said the relic was a glass feather? What if the Guardian is an eagle, not a person? We'd just need to follow it to its nest and then we'd find the relic,' Pippin chirps.

I shake my head. 'It's too obvious. There's no way the Guardian would leave such an easy clue. And an eagle's nest doesn't sound a very safe hiding place. Particularly not for something made of glass.'

'True, that's a problem with my theory. I'm always breaking things, and I've got fingers not talons,' Pippin says, waggling the toes of her sockless foot in the air.

'Snow eagles are almost extinct, so there aren't that many in the world. Maybe we should check their nests, just to be sure,' Aria says.

Pippin perks up. 'We can track them.'

'They're birds, not animals. They don't leave a handy trail of snapped twigs and dung we can track,' I say.

'Duh,' Pippin groans. 'I meant we can see them, up in the sky, then follow them from the ground.'

Again, I shake my head. 'They fly too fast for us. And they go in straight lines. You know the phrase "*as the crow flies*" – well it applies to eagles too. We might have to go across rivers and over mountains and through forests. All sorts of obstacles would be in our way.'

Aria's shoulders sag. 'Then we've got nothing.'

'Not nothing,' I say. 'Just because I don't think the star will lead us straight to a nest with the relic safely tucked inside, doesn't mean it isn't a clue. What do we know about snow eagles? There must be something about them in your books.'

Aria pulls a stack of books from the cupboard and spreads them out across her bed. 'Take your pick.'

One after another, we flick though the books. Garden birds, water birds, migrating birds, a whole book on penguins. Pippin waddles across the room squawking like a penguin.

The pile shrinks.

Eventually, Pippin drops the last book onto the floor. She flops onto her bed, dangles her head over the edge, and drums her heels against the wall. 'How can you have so many books on birds, but not a single one on eagles? Not even a chapter, not even a measly little paragraph.'

Aria shrugs.

'Right. Mum and Dad's room next,' I say, dragging the girls to their feet. 'Come on. I know most of their books are about travel, but they might have something. You never know.'

We tiptoe through the boat to Mum and Dad's cabin at the stern. Round portholes on each side of the room let the light stream in. Rows of bookshelves line the walls above the bed. A chair, dressing table, wardrobe, and a large wooden desk with brass trimmings are jammed into the corners of the room.

'I'll start on the port side, you two can work through the books on the starboard side,' I whisper.

'Why are we whispering?' Pippin asks.

'We're not supposed to be in here,' Aria hisses.

'Aren't we? Nobody told me.'

'Coz we assumed it was so obvious it didn't need to be said. Basic office rules, there's lots of customer stuff in here. Dad says it's safer for us not to know too much about his deliveries. Some of his customers can be rather … uhm … prickly about their privacy.'

'Oops. I often come in here. It's the best space to practise dancing,' Pippin says. She balances on one foot and attempts a pirouette. She stumbles, slips sideways, and crashes into the chair, landing in a heap on the floor.

Two of us freeze. Pippin, on the other hand, rolls around in a fit of laughter.

'Well that's it. They'll definitely have heard us now,' I sigh, waiting for a voice or footsteps. Silence.

'Whew, I think we got away with it,' Aria says. 'Hurry up. We'd better be quick with this search.'

Starting at the far end of the bookshelf, I run my fingers across the spines of the books, scanning their titles. Travel. Travel. Travel. History. I hesitate, that could be interesting, but it's not what I'm looking for today. My finger skips over to the next book. Travel …

I reach the end of the last shelf. 'There's nothing here. What about you?' I ask.

The girls shake their heads.

'What about the wardrobe?' Pippin asks, bouncing over to it. She turns the silver key and the doors spring apart. Clothes are crammed into every inch; there's never any wasted space on a boat. A few pairs of shoes are stacked neatly on the floor. 'Boring,' Pippin says, slamming it closed. She turns to the desk and tugs at the top drawer. 'Locked,' she grunts. She kneels in front of the keyhole and squints at it. 'I could pick this in a minute, I just need a hair pin.' She tips out a collection of rubbish from her pockets – string, an elastic band, a pencil – and waves a paperclip in the air. 'This is perfect.'

Aria frowns. 'We shouldn't.'

'They'll never know,' Pippin says. 'We can lock it again afterwards.'

'That's not the point,' Aria says, placing her hand over the keyhole.

'Pippin, just leave it. It's only the paperwork for the deliveries. Dad showed me once,' I say, opening another drawer and pulling out a wad of papers.

Aria scratches her head. 'I wonder why that drawer is locked when none of the others are.'

A flicker of doubt crosses my mind as I recall how Dad said he thought Sir Waldred had been through his papers. Curiosity gets the better of me, 'Well, I guess—'

Click. Before I have time to finish my sentence, Pippin pops the lock. Any lock that fails to deter a nine-year-old would be no obstacle at all to Sir Waldred. She glances up at us. 'Are you ready then? Let's see what the big secret is.'

Addressed in capital letters to Dad, is an envelope. It's been ripped open. Pippin pokes her nose inside it, then springs away, dropping the envelope as if stung by a bee.

'Careful,' Aria cries, picking it up.

'Sorry,' Pippin mumbles.

Aria sticks her hand into the brown envelope and pulls out the contents. A second envelope. This one is slender, the paper thin and crackly. On the front is written, *To Lady Philippa*. There's no address. Aria claps her hand to her mouth. 'That's the same handwriting as in the journal. It must have been written by the Air-Rider Guardian.'

'Why would Dad keep a letter from the Air-Rider Guardian secret? Do you think he's read it?'

'No way. You know the Number 1 rule of smuggling. *Never, ever, open a parcel.* It wouldn't matter what it was, he'd never open it.' Aria turns the envelope over. There, running the length of the back is a long, thin, razor-sharp cut. She peers inside. 'It's empty.'

My heart sinks. 'Oh no. I heard Dad tell Mum that he thought some papers were missing. I bet this is what he was talking about.'

Pippin grabs the envelope from Aria, shoves it back in the drawer, and slams it shut. 'That thing is trouble. We should put it back. Pretend we never found it.'

Aria squares her shoulders. 'No. We need to tell Dad it might have been written by the Air-Rider Guardian. And I want to ask him who Lady Philippa is.' She picks up the envelope and marches out of the room. Pippin hangs back. 'Come on, Pippin,' I call over my shoulder.

FOUR

TAKEN

Hands behind her back, Aria rocks on her heels. 'I know we shouldn't have been nosy, but we were trying to solve the bit in riddle about white eagles, so …' Her voice wavers. 'Well, we kind of went into your room. Just to check the books. I hope you aren't cross.'

'Not at all, they're books, they're meant to be read, but Mum and I don't have any books on birds. That's your department.'

'I know. We didn't find any, but we did find this …' She brings her hands forward and thrusts the envelope under his nose.

Dad turns pale. 'Where did you find that? It certainly wasn't on the bookshelves.'

'Uh, we kind of checked the whole cabin, not just the shelves. Anyway, I'm sure it was written by the Air-Rider Guardian, the handwriting is identical. Who did you get it from? Why was it in a locked drawer? Who's Lady Philippa? Why—'

'Slow down, Aria, that's a whole lot of questions.' Dad says. 'We'll come back to *why* you opened a locked drawer later, although I can probably guess *who* did it.' He raises an eyebrow at Pippin. 'Don't think I'll forget about that. For now, I'll do my best to answer your questions, but one at a time.'

'OK. Who's Lady Philippa?'

'One of the elders.'

'Which one?'

'The one who gave you the journal.'

'Her? The bird-like one? Why do we have a letter, or at least an empty envelope, addressed to her on board? We just saw her at the castle, you could have delivered it then. Why didn't you?'

'Same way we have all the uncollected parcels – the delivery doesn't get made.'

'That makes no sense. She was right there, and you never miss a delivery. Why didn't you deliver it?'

'Trust me, I tried, but it's like it's jinxed. Every time I try to deliver it, it literally vanishes into thin air. When I went to get it, the drawer was empty. Just like last time. Honestly, you'd think it didn't want to be delivered. Blasted thing always turns up later, once we've left the port and are safely out at sea. I'm sure Lady Philippa thinks we've lost it.'

'How can it just vanish? You either put it in the drawer, or you put it somewhere else.'

'That's what your mum says. But I promise you, it vanishes. My first black mark as a smuggler. Bit of a shame. Wish I'd never picked it up. Of all the weird things we've moved, who'd have thought a simple letter would cause so much trouble. I'll be glad to be shot of it.'

'At least if it had vanished, that means Sir Waldred didn't take it,' Aria says.

'We-ell, unfortunately, I think he might have. As you discovered, we have the envelope but the letter is missing. We have to assume Sir Waldred stole the contents.' Dad's shoulders slump as he turns away and busies himself with the charts.

Conversation clearly over, Aria chews the end of her hair as we wander back to her room. She opens her mouth to speak several times, then closes it again. 'Come on, out with it,' I say. 'I can see you're thinking something.'

'You're right. But it's going to sound mad. You've got to promise not to laugh?'

'I promise.'

'OK, here goes then. I have a theory about the letter. Dad's not daft. If he says he didn't touch it, I believe him. He's got no reason to lie. He'd much rather deliver it and be done with it.' I nod and Aria continues, 'So, here's my theory. I don't think we're delivering it to the right person. You saw there's no address on the envelope, just a name. What if she's not the right Lady Philippa? I mean, there could be two, couldn't there? Philippa isn't an unusual name after all.'

'Not many Ladies, though,' Pippin says, sliding out from under her bunk.

'Pippin, you gave me a fright. I didn't know you were there. And what are you doing hiding under your bed, anyway?'

'It's my den,' she says, grabbing my hand. 'Do you want to see?' She drags me onto the floor, and I peer beneath it. She's built a nest with cushions and blankets, and a whole tin of biscuits. 'Never know when you might need to hide.'

Later that evening, chores done for the day, I'm at a loose end. Bored. 'Would you mind if I had a look at the rest of the journal, Aria?' I ask.

With a sigh, she pulls it from her pocket, 'Other than the riddle, there's not much in it. You're going to be sorely disappointed. Doodles and stuff. Most of the writing has been scribbled out. There's practically nothing left to read.'

Back in my cabin I shove a dirty T-shirt and some scrunched up socks off the bed, and flop down on top of the crumpled blankets. I chew my lip. *Could there be another a clue in the journal?* It's unlikely that

Aria would have missed anything. Still, my heart races as I open it.

Page after page of doodles. I study them, trying to uncover a hidden meaning, but they seem to be just a muddle of curls and swirls and squiggly lines. Big chunks have been scribbled out, so it's impossible to make any sense out of the text. It's a complete mess. Goosebumps prick at my skin. Something about this book is wrong. But what? With a shiver, I drop it on the bed, close my eyes and let my mind drift. *Why does the book feel so strange … so … evil?* A scary thought worms its way forward in my mind. Could it be leading us into a trap?

A wave slaps against the side of the boat. My eyes ping open. I must have dozed off. The journal lies beside me, the pages splayed open. The writing catches my eye. Then it hits me. I didn't imagine it. There *is* something wrong with the journal. Very wrong.

'Aria, Pippin,' I cry, barging into the girls' room. Two socks, one green and one yellow, waggle in the air in front of my nose. Pippin collapses into a giggling heap on the floor. The blood has rushed to her head and her face is as red as a beetroot.

'You made me fall over!' she protests.

'It's not my fault. How was I supposed to know you were right behind the door?'

Stretched out on her bed, Aria gazes at the ceiling, her eyes unfocused. She sits up. 'What's up, Finn?'

'Something's wrong with the journal. Or maybe not "wrong", but definitely weird.' I flick towards the end of the journal. 'Look, the handwriting for the riddle's completely different.'

Aria turns back a few pages then slaps her forehead. 'How did I not notice that? It's so obvious.'

'You know they say you can tell a lot about a person by their handwriting. The writing at the start is kind of solid and confident. It looks sort of *strong* with those nice rounded letters, all the t's neatly crossed and i's precisely dotted, as a teacher would say. But the writing for the riddle is finer, more delicate, drifting upwards like it's trying to fly off the page …'

Aria squints at the page and frowns. 'Two different people. The elders said that the Air-Rider Guardian wrote the journal, so who added the riddle?'

'Duh, you guys need to listen more carefully,' Pippin interrupts. 'The elders didn't say the Guardian *wrote* it. Their exact words were, *"This belonged to the Guardian"*. That's a completely different thing. All we know is the Guardian had it at some point.' Pippin slides into the splits, points her green and yellow socked toes, and throws her arms up in the air in triumph.

Aria scratches her head. 'She's right. Pippin, why didn't you say something earlier?'

'You didn't ask.'

'Humph. I wish the Guardian was here. At least you had Lisana to help you with the Sea-Tamer relic, I've got nobody.'

'You've got us,' I point out.

'You can't answer my questions. Anyway, I'm so confused now, I'm going to need a list to help me think,' Aria says. She digs out her notebook, opens it at a new page, and writes *"What we know"*. She chews the end of her pen and stares at the blank page. 'Where do I start?'

Pippin peers over her shoulder. 'Start with the easy bit – what we *don't* know.'

Aria flicks to a new page, writes *"What we don't know"*, and underlines it twice.

Pippin reels off a list, counting the questions on her fingers as she goes. 'We don't know who the writers are. We don't know who wrote what. We don't know why the journal was given away. We don't know what the Guardian had to do with the journal. We don't know what happened to the Guardian. Oh, and don't forget, there's all that stuff crossed out, which could be important, but we can't read it. That's an awful lot of questions. I'm going to need a biscuit … energy boost,' she says, vanishing beneath her bed to retrieve the biscuit tin.

Aria writes them down, numbering the points, one through to six. Six impossible questions. She sits back and frowns. After a few minutes, she turns back to the page headed "What we know" and writes, '1. The handwriting suggests the writer of the riddle was an Air-Rider.'

'Are you sure? How did you work that out?' I ask.

'To be honest, it's a guess, but it looks a bit like my writing – all floaty and airy. You did say you can tell a lot about a person from their writing.'

Pippin emerges from under the bunk, her mouth full of biscuit. 'Not exactly scientific,' she mumbles.

Aria's shoulders slump as she draws a line through her theory.

'We'll work through the questions one by one. Don't worry. You trust the elders, don't you?'

She nods. 'Course I do. And they gave me the journal, so I know it's meant to help us.'

My skin crawls, cold and clammy, as the feeling of something evil within the book washes over me again. *Are we sailing straight into Sir Waldred's hands?* A chill runs down my spine, but before I can mention my worries about whether it could be a trap, a voice cuts through the air. 'Finn. Aria. Pippin. Hurry up. Dinner's ready and it's getting cold. Don't forget to wash your hands.'

'Coming, I'm starving,' Pippin calls, skipping off.

Before we head through to the saloon for dinner, Aria shoves the notebook and pen into her pocket and tucks the journal under her pillow.

Brows knit in concentration, her face dark as thunder, Aria doesn't utter a word throughout the meal. 'Are you OK? What are you thinking?' I ask under my breath.

'I've had a thought,' she whispers. 'A scary thought. You know how Pippin asked why they gave the journal away. What if it wasn't *given*? What if it was *taken*?'

FIVE

CHARM

Days pass. Our research has stalled; we can only hope Spitbank Fort provides some answers. And to make it worse, the wind has dropped, leaving us wallowing in the water, crawling forward at a snail's pace. I winch the sails in a bit, trying to catch a few extra puffs of breeze, but there just isn't enough to fill them properly. 'A flappy sail is not a happy sail,' Dad jokes, but nobody smiles. Aria creates gusts of wind but can't sustain it for long enough to keep the speed up constantly. I make waves to push us along, but it's exhausting. We pour over the charts, plotting the best course, analysing the tides. As the date of the Cold Moon gets closer and closer and we limp slowly towards the fort, frustration and helplessness make us tetchy. Conversation dies.

On the morning of the Cold Moon itself, Pippin perks up. She points at a speck on the horizon and dashes to the bow, bouncing up and down with excitement. She shouts back to us, 'That's it! We're going to make it.' My muscles unwind as a tight knot of tension floods out of my body. Pippin chatters on, 'It's going to be really strange going back. I bet nobody has been there since we abandoned it. Oooh, do you think there'll be bats in my bedroom?'

Over the next few hours the speck grows. Despite years of neglect, the thick granite walls rise out of the sea, every bit as defiant today as when the fort was first built to protect England from invasion during the Old Wars. The sea, unhappy to be interrupted by this rude structure, smashes relentlessly on the base. Great clouds of white foam fly into the air. Isolated and impenetrable, I can see why Sir Waldred used it as a secret base.

Pippin clambers up the mast and into the crow's nest to get a better view. Beside me, Aria tugs my arm. 'There's something we need to do before we get there.' She uncurls her hand and I see a kasai Fire-Dancer charm, not a real one obviously, a gilt-painted replica, threaded onto a ribbon to make a necklace.

'Why have you got that?'

'Since Pippin's helping us, I thought we should make her an official Relic Hunter. I know she doesn't have the blood-magic, but it doesn't feel right to leave her out. We can pretend it's a real charm. Let's give her a membership ceremony.' She tilts her head to look up the mast. 'Pippin, are you busy?' she shouts.

'Not really,' Pippin calls down.

'We've got something for you.'

Pippin wrinkles her nose up, 'Oooh. What is it?'

'You'll have to come down and find out,' Aria says.

Quick as a flash, Pippin slides down the mast.

Aria walks over to her and puts her hands on her shoulders. 'We're making you a Relic Hunter,' she says, slipping the necklace over Pippin's head. 'I have my hyrshu charm, and Finn has his pirrfu charm. Now you have a kasai charm.'

Pippin looks at it. 'Thanks, it's lovely, even if it's not real dime gold.'

Aria's face falls. 'I didn't think you'd notice.'

'Oh, it's not easy to trick me, I've seen more than you can imagine. But don't be sad, I still love it!' As she tucks it under her shirt, I catch a glimpse of something else; a delicate strand of silver chain with a peculiar pendant on it. It looks old, the metal dull and tarnished. She quickly pushes it out of sight, gives Aria a hug, then bounds over to me, clasping me round the waist and squeezing as hard as she can. She lets me go of me then twirls round on her tiptoes.

Aria laughs. 'See, it suits you. You're just like a Fire-Dancer.'

'What do you mean *like* a Fire-Dancer? Maybe I *am* a Fire-Dancer,' Pippin says indignantly.

Aria smiles. 'Of course, you are. And now you're officially a Relic Hunter too, so that means we're ready.'

I survey the fort. 'Dad, there's no jetty to tie up on.'

Pippin frowns. 'There used to be.'

Dad scratches his head. 'Maybe it got washed away by a storm. Whatever, we can't risk going any closer than this. The sea's far too rough, *The Alcina* will get smashed on the rocks. We'll have to come up with a new plan to get you there.'

'There's no time to make another plan. If we don't go now, Aria will miss the Cold Moon. Can we take the dinghy? It's not too far to row. I can do it.'

Dad frowns. 'It might be the only option, but with this rough sea, we mustn't overload it. Some of us will have to stay behind. You need Pippin to get you into the observatory, and Aria to read the signs, so that leaves ...'

I cut in, 'No way. I'm not staying behind.'

'I'd assumed you'd want to help them, Finn. Mum can stay with me. We'll take *The Alcina* into a quiet harbour where nobody will ask questions, hide there for the night and come back to pick you up at first light tomorrow. I'm trusting you to look after everyone.'

'I will.'

'Be careful. If there's any trouble, and I mean any trouble at all, let off one of these flares and we'll come straight back. We'll be on look-out all night.' He pulls out a bundle of emergency flares from the safety equipment locker, checks the date stamps to make sure they're safe to use, and hands them over. I tuck them into my backpack.

'I still can't see how you're going to get in,' Mum says as we complete another lap. 'There's no obvious entrance. It must be well hidden behind the sea defences.'

We start a third circle.

'There,' Aria says. I screw up my eyes and follow her finger. An uneven column of thin, rusty metal rails scale the wall.

'Good spot. We can tie the dinghy up at the bottom and climb the ladder.' Luckily, none of us are scared of heights.

'It doesn't look very safe. Several of the steps are missing,' Mum says, frowning. 'I'm not happy with this. Are you sure you can manage on your own? Maybe I should come too ...'

'We'll be fine. It's not so high really, we'll be up in a flash. We'll rope ourselves together for safety.' I hop off *The Alcina* into the dinghy, followed by Aria. As Pippin clambers over the guard rail, a choppy wave catches us and jerks the rowing boat away. She loses her balance and slips, plunging into the sea. Another wave bumps us back towards the boat. We're going to crush her. I grasp the oars and pull away as hard as I can to make some space.

Aria leans over the side of the dinghy and holds out her hand. 'Grab me,' she cries. Pippin's fingers slip through her grasp as she's swept away.

'I can't reach you.' Her voice is lost amongst the sound of the waves. The swirling sea pulls her about in a wild zigzag, like a rag doll. Mum flings the lifebelt into the sea. Pippin takes a few strokes of front crawl, then sinks beneath the waves. My eyes scan the surface for her, but the water is too murky.

Using my Sea-Tamer ability, I call out for any nearby fish to come and help, but there's no reply. After centuries of overfishing, the sea is empty. A small head pops up in the middle of the lifebelt. She pulls herself through and tucks it under her arms. She kicks out towards us but the current whisks her twenty metres further out to sea. Telltale white lines slice through the water around her; a rip current. I push against it, but the sea resists me. Cursing my lack of Sea-Tamer training, I yell at Pippin. 'You're in a rip. You won't be able to beat it. It's too strong, even for me. Swim across it at an angle. It's the only way. Once you're free, it'll be easier I promise. Then head for the fort. We'll try to get behind you.'

Still clinging to the orange ring, Pippin turns across the current. Strong, smooth kicks. Not for the first time, her confidence in the water strikes me.

'Wow. She's a good swimmer, especially for an Earth-Wanderer,' Aria says, echoing my thoughts.

Free from the vicious clutches of the rip, Pippin makes progress towards the fort. 'That's it, well done, Pippin. You're clear. Now head for the shore. We're coming.'

'Finn, give me the oars,' Aria says, taking them out of my hands without waiting for a reply. 'You need to focus on Pippin. She's going to get battered on the rocks in a minute.'

I try again to control the sea, this time it relents to my power. I concentrate on cushioning the water around Pippin. Finally, she drags herself out of the water onto the base of the fort, still clutching the lifebelt, her long dark hair plastered to her head. Perched on a rocky outcrop, her tiny, bedraggled, body looks so fragile. With a big grin, she gives us the thumbs up.

Aria rows up to the fort and I tie the dinghy onto a heavy iron ring drilled into the wall next the base of the ladder. Encrusted with barnacles, it clearly hasn't been used for a while. I give it a tug to check it's secure, I wouldn't want to lose the dinghy. Rust flakes off in great chunks, but it holds firm.

Dad swings the wheel and *The Alcina* turns away from us, heading towards the harbour. Mum runs to the stern of the boat. 'Be careful. I'll be looking for you at first light tomorrow.' She blows us a big kiss and waves madly, her white hair flying in the wind.

As the boat heads off into the sunset, we're alone with nothing but the wind and the waves. The stone walls of the fort loom over us. Rung by rung, we climb into the unknown.

SIX

DISASTER

Standing on top of the battlements, we survey the fort. Narrow stone steps creep down the inside of the wall. 'Lead the way, Pippin,' I whisper.

'You don't need to whisper,' she says. 'It's deserted. We all left together.'

'But what if they came back?'

The colour seeps from Pippin's cheeks. Aria draws her bow and nocks an arrow, and, one after another, we tiptoe down the steps. I look around. Although the fort looks enormous from the outside, once you're inside the thick stone exterior walls it's actually quite cramped. Assorted small buildings are scattered around the central courtyard. Weeds poke through cracks in the paving slabs. A tattered remnant of curtain flaps in an open window, bleached pale pink by the sun. A terracotta plant pot lies on its side, broken. It's flanked by two other pots, their contents brown and brittle. Seagulls circle overhead, squawking noisily at the intrusion.

A shadow flickers across the courtyard. We flatten ourselves against the exterior wall. 'Did you see that?' Aria asks, her eyes are wide.

'Probably just a rat,' I whisper.

Gravel crunches underfoot.

'That's too heavy for a rat. Someone's here. We need to hide. Now.'

'This way,' Pippin hisses. She scurries behind a pile of stones with us close on her heels, barely hidden.

'What do we do now?' Aria's voice wavers.

I edge myself up onto my elbows and peak over the top of the stones. The courtyard seems empty. I sink back to the ground. 'We can't stay here. We're too exposed. We need to get inside one of the buildings, then we can make a plan. On the count of three, make a run for that one.' I point at the nearest door.

'What if it's locked?' Aria asks.

'Good point. The window's broken. I'll go first and you wait here. If the door's locked, I'll clear the glass away then we can climb through. Wait for my signal.'

In a low crouch, I scurry across the courtyard towards the door, praying it's unlocked. Something shoots out in front of me. I trip. By the time I'm back on my feet, whatever it was has vanished. No time to lose now. Abandoning the crouch, I sprint towards the door. Please be unlocked. The handle turns. I spin round to gesture to the girls to wait while I check it's safe, but it's too late, they're both running already. They charge into the room and I slam the door behind us. Inside, we lean against the door, panting. On one side of the room is a chest of drawers, its moth-eaten contents tipped on the floor. Beside it, a wardrobe, the doors flung open, tattered coats still on their hangers. In the far corner is a dusty bookcase with half-full shelves, the books scattered around the floor.

'Something's out there,' Aria says.

We back away from the door into the corner and crouch behind the bookcase. A flicker of movement outside the broken window catches my eye. I put my arm out in front of Aria and Pippin and we freeze. My heart races. A shape appears, silhouetted against the bright light outside.

Aria screams.

The shadow edges over the broken glass and leaps down with a loud miaow. I let out a sigh of relief, it's only a cat. It darts over to Pippin, winding itself round her legs, purring like crazy.

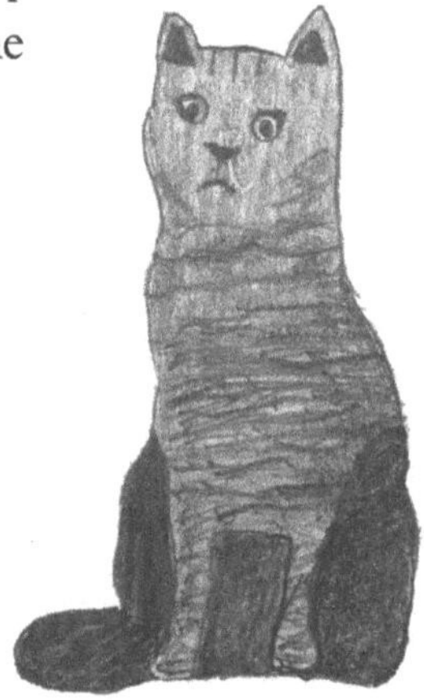

Pippin picks it up and smothers it with kisses. She turns to us, cradling the cat in her arms. Her eyes brim with tears. 'This is Hobnob. I can't believe he's alive. The day we left, I couldn't find him. Sir Waldred wouldn't wait. He said the boats were going, with or without me, and with or without Hobnob. He was only a kitten.' Tears splash down her cheeks. She wipes them away with the back of her hand.

'How did he survive all on his own with nobody to feed him?' Pippin asks.

'Mice. They've had the run of the place. He's done all right, I reckon.' I scratch his tummy. 'He's clearly not starving, is he?'

'He is a bit fatter than when I last saw him,' Pippin admits. A steady buzz comes from her arms.

'That's not a purr, it sounds like he's drilling,' I joke.

Pippin beams. 'I think he missed me.'

'Well, he seems very healthy. And the good news is, we've found our stalker. I think the fort is deserted, other than for Hobnob that is.'

We open the door and step out into the twilight. A warm breeze blows through the weeds, rustling them like a summer meadow.

'Right, Pippin, where's this telescope then?'

Arms still full of cat, she nods her head towards a small, windowless, white-washed building with a copper domed roof, turned mint-green by the weather. It looks out of place in the middle of a military fort. 'That's the observatory.' We walk towards it. Pippin passes Hobnob to Aria, drops onto her hands and knees, and starts crawling around, picking up loose stones and scrabbling underneath them.

'Come on, you two. Help me find the key, will you?'

'Why's it locked?' Aria asks. 'It's not as if you're going to get burgled out here.'

Pippin tilts her head to the side and wrinkles her nose up. 'Nobody other than Sir Waldred was ever allowed in there,' she says.

I chuckle. 'Nobody? I'm guessing you completely ignored that rule, otherwise, you wouldn't know there's a telescope.'

Pippin giggles. A few minutes later, she prises a small brass key out of the dirt with her fingernails, rubs the muck off, and wipes her hands on her shirt, leaving a muddy smear down the front. Aria winces. She sits back on her heels and holds the key up. 'Knew it would be here somewhere.'

The three of us cluster in front of the door. Pippin puts the key in the lock and turns it. The latch clicks. She pauses.

'Are you ready to solve this mystery?'

Pippin turns the handle and pushes the heavy steel door open. Inside, it's dark and gloomy. A gust of wind catches the door. It slams on my fingers. Bones crunch and a sharp pain shoots up my arm. 'Ouch,' I yelp, cradling my throbbing hand.

'Are you OK?' Aria asks.

'Yeah. I'm fine,' I say, not wanting to worry her. I turn my back on them and try to flex my fingers. Not good. Gingerly, I pull my sleeve down over my hand and rejoin the girls. In the centre of the room, a cloth is draped over a large object. Pippin whisks the cloth off and drops it in a heap on the floor. 'Da da …' she proclaims, taking a bow like a magician after revealing his trick.

I step back. Rather awestruck, we approach the telescope in silence. Balanced on a tripod, it's a huge brass tube. Levers and knobs of all sizes stick out like some kind of crazy porcupine. 'Wow it's beautiful,' I say. 'How old is it?'

'It's an antique. It's got to be hundreds of years old. Sir Waldred stole it from Marseille and snuck it back here. Said it was no use to them coz there was too much light pollution.'

'Hmmm. Bet they'd like it back; we should tell them it's here,' I say. 'Aria, do you know how to use it?'

'Yes,' Aria says, although her voice wavers. 'Kind of.'

Pippin hops from foot to foot, 'Oooh, I do, I do.'

A large black remote control on a heavy cable dangles down the wall. Pippin pushes a button and the dome splits apart. She twiddles a few levers then swings the telescope up towards the sky.

'Good to go now, over to you, Aria.'

As Aria adjusts the angle of the telescope, Pippin pushes another button and the dome rotates to align with the telescope.

'And?' I ask, cradling my swollen hand. 'Can you see anything?'

'Give me a chance,' Aria snaps. 'I don't even know what I'm looking for.' She spins the telescope. Pippin pushes another button, holding it down while the dome rotates to match. Clearly, she's spied on Sir Waldred. I wonder if he knew she was watching.

Aria mutters to herself as she works methodically across the sky, scanning it inch by inch through the telescope. Pippin fidgets, until she can no longer contain herself. 'Can I see? Can I have a turn?' she chirps, bouncing up and down beside Aria.

'Let Aria finish first. Then we can both have a look,' I say.

Eventually, Aria stands back. 'There's nothing unusual at all. I don't understand. I thought there would be a message in the sky.'

'Do you think we made a mistake with the prophecy? Did we read it wrong?' I ask.

'No. The prophecy was quite clear. I must be missing something.' Aria squares her shoulders and takes up the telescope again. Silence fills the room. Even Pippin stops jigging about.

With a gasp, Aria steps back, blinks hard, then glues her eye back to the lens.

'What? What did you see?' Pippin cries. Startled by the first shout he's heard in years, Hobnob leaps from Pippin's arms. She dives after the cat, knocking the telescope in the process. It wobbles. I lurch for it but, with my balloon-sized injured hand, fumble. The telescope lands with a crash. Shards of glass spray across the floor.

SEVEN

STAR

'No! Pippin, look what you did,' Aria wails. 'You're so clumsy. Why are you always in such a rush?'

Pippin scrambles on the floor, heaving the telescope back up. 'It was an accident. It's probably fine.'

'It's not fine,' Aria says, pointing to the pieces of glass scattered at our feet. Tears splash down her cheeks. 'It's broken. What are we going to do now?'

'It was only a little bit of glass that fell out …' Pippin says peering down the lens. She sticks a finger in the end.

'Stop. Don't do that,' Aria cries. 'You'll only make it worse.'

Rather sheepishly, Pippin steps away from the telescope, shoves her hands in her pockets, and rocks backwards and forwards on her heels.

I brush the shards of glass away from the lens

with the corner of my shirt. Although there's a crack, it's not completely shattered, it might still work. 'Give it a go,' I say, stepping aside. My heart races as I watch Aria cradle the telescope in her hands and pull it towards her eye. 'Well? Does it still work?' I ask.

'Sort of,' Aria says. She refocuses the telescope, her brows knit together. 'Some of the stars are a bit fuzzy where the lens is damaged, but I think the rest of it is OK. We're lucky the mirror didn't break. That would have been a killer.' Suddenly, she stands bolt upright. 'I've got it! Come on, you need to see this. It's amazing.'

I look through the telescope. A million stars sparkle, although there's a rather annoying blurry patch in one corner. 'What am I looking for? A new star?'

'No, not a star,' Aria says, beaming. 'A whole new constellation.'

'A new constellation? That's impossible,' I say.

'Absolutely. It's shaped like a hyrshu charm. And it just appeared. Right in front of my eyes. One minute it wasn't there. And the next it was.'

I check my watch. Midnight.

I stare into the telescope again, letting my mind gather the stars into constellations – Orion and his Belt, The Plough, The Little Bear – until I spot a cluster of stars which could be linked together to make a shape like a hyrshu charm. She's right. It's squint, tilted to one side, but unmistakeable. I step back, grinning from ear to ear.

'Your turn now,' Aria says to Pippin. 'It's OK, I'll hold the telescope for you.'

Pippin tiptoes forward and stops with her feet well back from the tripod and her hands crossed behind her back. She sticks her head forward, so she looks like a duck.

I stare up at the sky through the open roof of the observatory while Aria shows Pippin the constellation. 'What does it mean?' I ask.

Aria scratches her head. 'Not sure. You see the brightest star in the hyrshu constellation? Well, that star is somewhere over Asia. I reckon it's pointing to where the Air-Rider relic is hidden. Just like a pirrfu charm helped you find the Sea-Tamer relic, it seems a hyrshu charm will lead us to its relic. I'll have to use the astrolabe to show me more precisely where.'

She pulls a brass astrolabe, a complicated mechanical clock-like object, from her pocket. The intricate engravings on its case are almost completely worn away from years of use. She flips it open and starts taking measurements from the stars.

'Will you be able to remember everything?' Pippin asks.

'I think so,' Aria says, but her voice wavers.

Pippin screws up her nose. 'Why don't you draw a map?' From a broken wooden desk, she produces an ink pen and some slightly damp paper.

Aria carefully plots each of the stars, linking them together with a thin line to form the outline of a hyrshu charm, and adds the nearby, familiar, Orion constellation with the bright star Bellatrix, then the Gemini constellation with Pollux and Castor. A few ink blotches form on the soggy paper.

One section of the drawing remains blank, the patch where the lens is damaged and the stars are fuzzy.

'Can you remember anything about that section from when you first looked, Aria?' I ask, crossing my fingers.

Aria shakes her head.

'Sorry,' Pippin mumbles, her gaze fixed on the floor. 'It's going to be my fault if we can't find the relic, isn't it?'

'It was an accident. But maybe next time you could be just a little bit more careful and not rush so much?'

Pippin shuffles her feet and nods.

Aria works on her map, adding details and notes, switching between peering through the telescope and scribbling on the paper. Eventually, she pushes the telescope aside and the pen grinds to a halt. 'I can't do any more,' she says. 'The hyrshu constellation just vanished.'

I check my watch, twelve minutes past midnight on the twelfth day of the twelfth month. Twelve. We get our powers when we turn twelve, we say we're on cloud twelve when we're happy, cats have twelve lives. It can't be a coincidence. Fingers crossed Aria got enough details down, as the more I think about it, the more I'm convinced this is not an annual occurrence. I think it had to be today, and only today. The Cold Moon won't fall on the twelfth of December again for many years.

A chill wind swirls around the observatory. Pippin pushes a button and the dome closes over our heads.

'Let's get some sleep,' Pippin suggests. 'We've still got a few hours before daybreak. We can stay in my old bedroom. Sir Waldred made us leave in such a rush, we just abandoned everything, so my bed will still be there.'

'Why did you leave in such a hurry?'

'Sir Waldred was summoned.'

'Summoned? By who?' I can't imagine anyone being bold enough to "summon" Sir Waldred. He usually does the summoning.

'How should I know,' Pippin snaps.

She leads us across the courtyard into another room. A few battered pieces of furniture are pushed up against the wall.

'Give me a hand,' she says, tugging at a huge brass bed, piled high with bedding. 'I have to warn you, it's not like my bed on *The Alcina*. It's really hard and lumpy.' Together, we heave it into the middle of the room. A musty aroma wafts from the blankets as we spread them out, but they feel dry enough. The bed's huge and there's loads of room for the three of us.

'Wake me up if you see any bats,' Pippin says.

'You weren't joking, Pippin. This must be the lumpiest mattress in the world,' Aria says as she climbs in, but Pippin has already curled up into a ball and is snoring away.

Eventually I hear Aria's breathing relax as she falls asleep. I lie flat on my back, watching shadows crawl across the ceiling as the silver moonlight filters through the curtain-less window, not daring to move a muscle in case I wake the girls.

'Wake up, wake up.'

Ouch. I open one eye. Pippin's pummelling my chest. I must have nodded off eventually, but I didn't sleep well and feel groggy. I drag myself upright, while Pippin shakes Aria awake.

'Come on,' she urges. 'It's daybreak. We need to go now. I can see *The Alcina*. It's nearly here.'

'Just as well one of us has a good internal alarm clock. How long have you been up?' I ask.

'A while. I went for a walk. Can Hobnob come with us?' Pippin's eyes have a new sparkle to them.

'Why not? I don't reckon Mum and Dad will mind,' I say. 'Every ship needs a ship's cat.'

Pippin tucks the cat into her backpack, leaving his head peeking out at the top, sprints out of the chamber and bounds up the stone staircase. She's halfway up before Aria and I even reach the bottom step. At the top, she steps onto the wide stone battlements. 'Hurry up. The boat's here.' She starts to climb down the iron ladder.

'Wait for us,' I cry.

Pippin plonks herself on the ledge, swinging her feet over the parapet until we reach the top. We organise ourselves so Aria goes down first, followed by Pippin. With my injured hand, it's difficult to hold onto the ladder properly and I have to brace my body each time I move down a rung. Aware of my injury, I'd decided not to rope us together for the descent and, in the excitement, both Pippin and Aria forgot to do it. I didn't remind them; it was a call between my own safety and putting Aria and Pippin in more danger. If I'd told them about my hand, they'd have insisted.

Halfway down, a rusty iron bar crumbles beneath my right foot. I plummet, jerking to a stop, almost ripping my arm from the shoulder socket. My toes scrabble against the wall, trying to find a foothold. I cling on with my one good hand, cursing my injury. Millimetre by millimetre, my fingers start to slide from the bar.

I find a foothold.

'Got you!' Pippin calls. I look down. My foot has landed right on top of her head.

'Oops, sorry,' I say.

'It's OK, I've got a very thick skull,' she says. 'Sir Waldred was always telling me that.'

'I don't think he meant that as a compliment,' I say. 'He's a bully. He was being mean to you.'

'Oh. I did wonder if it was a good thing or not. Doesn't matter, I ignored him anyway. It *is* a bit uncomfortable though, so do you think you could find a proper step soon?'

'Sorry,' I say again, removing my foot and putting it back on a rung.

Testing each step before I put my weight on it, I reach the bottom of the ladder. The dinghy bumps against the rocky platform and I cringe at the scraped paint. Aria unties it from the iron ring and picks up the oars. The current pushes us away from the fort.

Back aboard *The Alcina*, Mum squints at Pippin's backpack. 'Who's this?' she asks, as Hobnob's head pokes out from the top.

'This is Hobnob. He's mine, from when I was little,' Pippin says. 'Is it OK to keep him on the boat?'

Mum scratches Hobnob under his chin and he purrs. 'Of course.' She turns to me. 'Finn, why are you clutching your hand? Let me see.'

'My fingers got caught in a door. I think they may be broken.'

Aria gasps. 'You should have said.'

'Can you wriggle them?' Mum asks. I wince with pain. 'Better get a splint on right away.'

EIGHT

CHASE

Aria carefully transfers her notes onto the maps. 'No matter how I look at it, the hyrshu constellation is pointing at the Himalayan mountains.'

Dad peers over Aria's shoulder. 'It's not going to be easy journey. We'll have to sail across the Bay of Biscay, and then we have three choices for where to start the overland trek from. The first option would be to sneak through the Suez Canal ...'

Mum sits bolt upright. 'That's not a choice. The Suez Canal is a death sentence. There's no way to slip through that narrow channel unseen.' She shudders. 'What's the second option?'

'Sail to New Damascus.'

Mum frowns. 'That's not much better! New Damascus is the Earth Lords' eastern capital. It's every bit as dangerous as New London.'

'I know,' Dad says. 'But the last option is to sail across the Black Sea, and that's patrolled by jet-ships. Shall we have a family vote? Anyone for the Suez Canal?'

Everyone shakes their head.

'New Damascus?'

Pippin's hand shoots up. Aria rolls her eyes.

'What? Why are you all looking at me like that?' Pippin says. 'I lived in New London for years. I liked it. If New Damascus is like that, it sounds fine to me.'

'Yes,' I say. 'But you were fine because you were with Sir Waldred at the time. It's a bit different for us. If you recall, Sir Waldred is trying to kill us. Last time we were in New London, we only just escaped with our lives.'

'Suppose so,' she says, lowering her hand.

'Black Sea route?'

Given the other options, there's really no choice. I raise my hand. Three other hands creep into the air too. Pippin shrugs and raises hers.

'That's decided then,' Dad says.

'What happens after we cross the Black Sea?' I ask, my voice wavering as I picture trekking into the mountains. I've never been more than a few miles inland and, even then, I could still see or hear the sea.

'We'll pick up an old trader route, the Silk Route, and pretend to be merchants. It should help us avoid any difficult questions.'

'Can we go on a steam train?' Pippin squeals, bouncing up and down with excitement. 'I've never been on one.'

'You're in luck then, we'll take a steam train for the first part of the journey, but once we start heading up into the mountains, we'll need to hike. It's a shame we can't get through the Suez Canal,' Dad says, scratching his head. 'It would be much quicker—'

'Ragnar, don't even think it,' Mum says firmly. 'It's simply not an option.'

'I know.' Dad closes the charts with a sigh.

Later, I pull Dad aside. 'What about our documents? Won't crossing those borders flag us to the Earth Lords?'

'Don't worry. I'll reach out to a few friends and sort us entry permits.'

'Do you trust them to keep our trip secret?'

'I'd trust them with my life.'

With the route decided, there's no point hanging around. After a few days, I take the splint off and wriggle my fingers. They feel fine, Mum was right, it was just a bad bruise.

The first few weeks are uneventful but as we approach the Bay of Biscay the waves change from long smooth rollers into sharp choppy wedges, crashing against each other in a never-ending battle. Dad paces up and down the boat. 'It's getting very rough. There must be a big storm out there.' All the bad weather from the Atlantic Ocean ends up here, and the waves get scrunched together. If Dad's right, it could get worse. 'I knew we shouldn't be making this crossing in winter; this sea has claimed far bigger ships than ours.'

'Should we stick closer to the coast?' I ask.

'For safety, we'll have to. The voyage will take us longer, but this sea is so treacherous I'd be a whole lot happier if we were nearer to the shore.'

Dad was right about the waves building. He calls a boat meeting. 'Better prepare for a bumpy journey. Batten down the hatches, secure the lines, and stay below deck unless it's essential. Lifejackets on, and nobody moves without clipping onto one of the safety lines.'

Even closer to land, the boat gets tossed about like clothes in a washing machine. Monstrous waves batter us from all sides. I try to use my ability to clear a path through the water, but my head throbs from the constant effort.

'Have a rest, Finn. There's a long way to go,' Dad says. 'Mum and I will take it for a bit.'

Too exhausted to argue, I crawl to my cabin and drag myself into bed, fix the lee cloth down the side so I don't fall out as the boat bounces around, and close my eyes. Next thing I know, I'm woken by a crash as we're hit by a wave, and the boat is knocked sideways. I grab the lee cloth and wait for the boat to right itself, but it doesn't. It keeps falling. Someone screams. Aria, or Pippin, or both? I can't tell. The boat heels further over. We're too far gone, there's no way back now, we're going to capsize. I brace myself. A swoosh of water floods inside. An almighty bang, and the world turns upside down. I smack onto the roof of my cabin. Then it goes dark.

I come to and rub my eyes. With a sigh of relief, I realise we're not upside down, the weight of the keel must have pulled us back upright after the capsize. But that's the only good news. We're sinking. Water sloshes around my cabin floor. Clothes, a book, my toothbrush, and a single flip-flop slop against each other in the water. I sit up and rub my head.

'Mum? Dad? Aria? Pippin?' Silence. The icy water comes up to my knees as I wade through the debris. 'Mum? Dad? Aria? Pippin?'

I stick my head outside. The boat is wrecked, the mast bent over like a felled tree, snapped in the middle, the top trailing into the sea, forcing the boat to list over to the side. Dad's at the stern. I grab a lifejacket and clip on. Clambering over the tangled mess of ropes and wires towards him, I shout, 'Is everyone OK?'

'Mum's injured, but I've got her into our cabin. The girls are looking after her.'

'What happened?'

'We got hit by a freak wave. It came right out of nowhere. We rolled.'

'What can I do to help?'

'We need to get the mainsail in, it's trailing in the sea beneath us like a giant parachute brake. Here, take these.' He passes me some wire cutters. I get to work. With the rigging and lines cleared, we heave the soaking sail onboard and shove it in a locker. He wipes his brow and goes over to what's left of the mast. 'Hold this steady for me while I saw it off.' He hacks at the remains and we push it overboard, watching it float away like a broken matchstick.

'What are we going to do now, Dad? We obviously can't sail.'

'We'll have to head in for repairs. There's a lot of work to do. We'll need a new mast ...' His voice trails off.

'Sorry, Dad.'

'It's not your fault.'

'No, I mean I'm sorry about *The Alcina*. She's ruined.'

'It's all fixable. I'm just glad everyone's OK.'

While Dad sets up a jerry rig, I grab a bucket and start bailing the water out. Mum insists she's fine, despite the pain etched into her face, and sends Aria and Pippin to help bail. Although she hasn't said anything, I have a suspicion her injuries are a lot more serious than she's letting on.

Luckily, we'd come in pretty close to shore, so the nearest port is only a few hours away. As we limp towards it, Pippin disappears. Annoyed, I hunt for her. 'Pippin, where are you? Now's not the time to play hide and seek,' I shout.

Her head pops up over the bow of the boat. 'Over here.' I hang over the side to see what she's up to. Her legs are wrapped round a rope which she's tied to a cleat and dangles down into the water. She has a paintbrush in one hand and waves it at her artwork: *The Alcina* now reads *The Afdiha*. 'Do you like it? We're in disguise.'

I nod. 'Good idea.'

Masquerading as *The Afdiha*, we approach the port, an ugly, industrial town where lines of dusty buildings crawl up the surrounding hillside in a futile attempt to escape. A factory spits out dirty grey fumes which make my eyes sting. Coughing and spluttering, I bring the boat into the mooring and Aria leaps ashore with the ropes. Nobody pays any attention, busy with the daily grind of work and survival.

'I'm going to find my old smuggler-friend, Javier, he'll be able to help. Wait here,' Dad says. 'Don't go exploring until we know it's safe.'

I scan the grey port: it holds no attraction. Dad reappears a few hours later on a horse and cart with a man who he introduces as Javier. I help them carry Mum off the boat and lie her down on a pile of blankets in the back of the cart. With Mum lying down, there's no room for us all in the back. 'We'll meet you at the hospital,' Dad says. 'Javier will show you the way.' At a click, the horse breaks into a trot.

Javier doesn't say as much as we hurry along after him. By the time we arrive, Dad's waiting in the lobby. He whisks us up to see Mum. She's propped up on a pile of pillows, her skin as white as the sheets. A clipboard hangs at the end of the bed, with a strange name on it. Dad catches me looking at it and puts his fingers to his lips. 'Shhh. Javier sorted us out with fake identities,' he whispers.

A doctor in a white coat comes over to us. Grim-faced, he ushers us into a private room.

'Your mum is really strong. You'll be glad to hear we've managed to get her comfortable. Unfortunately, it will be a while before the full extent of her injuries are clear. She's going to need a lot of care and treatment over the coming months. I'm sorry, but I do need to warn you, there is a chance that her injuries could be very severe and may never heal properly.'

'What do you mean?' Aria asks.

'The worst-case situation is that she might be paralysed from the waist down. If that's the case, even with intensive physiotherapy, she may never be able to walk again.'

NINE

RECOVERY

Aria bursts into tears and Dad hugs her tight. 'Don't worry,' Dad says. 'Whatever happens, nothing will stop your mum from living her life to the maximum. We'll let the doctors do their job and take it from there.'

The doctor leans forward. 'Don't jump to conclusions, there's a long way to go before we're there. And with treatment, there's a good chance she'll make a full recovery.'

Over the next few weeks, the doctors run more tests on Mum while we ping between doing repairs at the boatyard and visiting her at the hospital. Although the boat makes steady progress, Mum doesn't. The doctors suggest moving her into a larger hospital about six hours' ride away where a full-time team of physiotherapists will put her through a rigorous programme of exercises. I know

Dad wants to go with her, and Aria too, so I offer to stay and supervise the boat repairs. Unable to decide, Pippin tosses a coin and ends up with me.

Relocation day arrives. The nurses put Mum into a horse-drawn wagon then Dad and Aria clamber into the back with her. Once they've gone, Pippin and I trudge back to the boat in silence. I try to cheer her up with a trip to the market to choose some fruit and vegetables for supper, but her heart isn't in it.

'It doesn't feel right here without them,' she says.

'I know, but Mum needs the best care we can get her.'

Weeks become months, and slowly but surely *The Alcina,* still disguised as *The Afdiha,* starts to look like her old self. A new mast has been fitted, the auburn varnish gleams in the summer sunlight. Finally, the boat is ready, but Mum isn't. One hot day, Dad comes back to inspect the repair work. Satisfied the boat is seaworthy again, he calls a family meeting to discuss what we should do: stay here until Mum is fit, or leave Mum behind. Neither option appeals. We vote, putting slips of paper into a hat. Dad pulls an extra slip from his pocket, Mum's vote, and adds it to the hat. I hold my breath as we count them. Two votes each, with one slip left to draw. Dad smooths the final scrap of paper on the table. And there it is, we're moving on. We make one last trip to the hospital. Mum reels off a list of forty things we have to remember to do, including brushing our teeth, and makes us promise to write to her.

Back on the boat, Dad digs out all the charts. In front of us, the Bay of Biscay sparkles in the sun, still choppy, but without the urgent violence of winter.

It feels good to be moving again, and back on the quest, so even though we miss Mum, there's a buzz in the air. After hiding for months behind our assumed identities, we've relaxed our guard. We still keep a look-out, but the schedule slips, we forget whose turn it is, the gaps between shifts expand from minutes to hours. I doze off during one of my shifts. A loud noise over the gentle splash of the waves on the hull jolts me awake. Too late, we spring into action. A black jet-ship roars over the horizon towards us. Trackers.

'Finn, you were supposed to be on watch. This is all your fault,' Aria shrieks.

'How did they find us? All the power is off, isn't it?' Dad says.

Pippin's hand flies up to her mouth. 'The air jet! I forgot to switch it off. Sorry.'

'Sorry doesn't help now,' Aria snaps. 'What shall we do? Can Finn hide us in a mist like he did in the Northern Seas?'

'A mist over the Northern Seas is perfectly normal,' Dad says, 'but it's too hot here. The sun would burn it away in minutes. It would look very suspicious.'

'Then what do you suggest?'

'Let them approach. Stick to the story, we're merchants on our way to pick up silk to take back to New London. Take our flag down and replace it with this, we should have done it before we set out, but what with everything else, I forgot.' He holds out a yellow traders' flag, the one that invites the authorities onboard to conduct an inspection.

'But if they board us, you know what they'll find. It won't take them long to realise we're smugglers.'

'We'll have to take our chances.'

With nowhere to hide, we watch them approach. 'Prepare for boarding,' a voice shouts across to us.

Aria springs to her feet. 'I have a plan.' She clenches her teeth and clasps her hands together. I watch a whirlwind zing to life between her palms. My heart sinks as I recognise the move, the one she can't do. Her brow furrows as she pulls her hands apart. The whirlwind zings faster and faster. A high-pitched screech erupts from the middle of the ball as she flings it into the water. It's going to fizzle out. My heart aches at the thought of the wave of disappointment that will spread over her face when it fails. But it doesn't, it twists and turns and grows, taking on the form and fury of a dragon.

Then the dragon tornado explodes, shredding the sea into pieces. My jaw drops.

Calm and collected, Aria turns to Dad. 'Sail into it,' she orders.

Dad turns the wheel and heads straight for the eye of the tornado. The boat spins. Faster and faster.

'Hold on,' Aria yells. *The Alcina* whirls round and round at a dizzying speed. I grab at the mast but miss. My fingertips clasp a rope. Dangling on the end, I swing wildly, trying to wrap my feet around it.

'Everyone OK?' Dad cries.

'I'm fine,' I say, forcing my eyes open.

'Me too,' Pippin says. 'And I've got Hobnob.' The cat clings onto her dress with his claws, his normally sleek hair standing on end and his green eyes as wide as saucers. I bet he's wondering why he left such a nice quiet life on the fort, filled with endless happy days chasing mice and sunbathing undisturbed on the rocks.

Far below us, the trackers have adjusted course to avoid the tornado and are heading in the opposite direction.

We're spinning through the clouds, higher and higher.

'Enough, Aria,' Dad cries. 'Don't go any higher. The boat can't take this much pressure. It'll rip into pieces. You need to relax. Count to three and breathe.'

'One. Two. Three.' The wild spin slows. 'Four. Five. Six.' We sink back towards the sea. 'Seven. Eight …' Falling. Faster. Down.

'Aria, focus! You're dropping us.'

'Sorry. I was counting to ten.'

'I said three. Three, not ten,' Dad yells.

Aria claps her hands together. The wind catches us and the free fall slows, just as we smack into the sea. The splash from our crash landing reaches the trackers, the jet-ship spins and roars back towards us. After that display, they'll never believe we're traders. *Think, Finn, think. How are we going to escape from this?* An idea takes shape in my head and a huge hole appears in the sea. *The Alcina* plunges down into the black depths.

Three faces turn and stare at me in horror.

'What have you done?' Aria cries. 'We're going to drown.'

'No, we won't,' I say. I raise my arms above my head and clap my hands together. Water rushes over our heads, enclosing us in a bubble. Through the roof of the bubble, we watch the jet-ship.

'It's going to sail right over us,' Pippin cries, dancing a jig.

'Not bad both of you, and without training,' Dad says, smiling.

Far above us, the crew of the jet-ship line up along the side of their boat, staring into the water, speechless.

A sharp voice cuts through the water. 'It's them. Don't let them escape.'

I know that voice. Sir Waldred!

Just as well we didn't try to bluff our way out of this as traders. Someone fires a harpoon. It bounces off the roof of our bubble-cave, slides down the side, and sinks to the seabed.

Sir Waldred shakes his fist at us. 'You won't escape. You'll have to come up at some point.'

'He's right,' Dad says. 'We can't sail beneath them forever.'

'I'll take care of them.' I make a circular movement with my hand. A large wave picks the jet-ship up and sweeps it away, the engines screaming in protest.

TEN

LAND

With the jet-ship gone, for now, I allow our bubble to float to the surface where it bursts with a gentle pop. Dad checks the air-jet is off, making us virtually invisible to radar, and we set off again. We reach the far side of the Black Sea with no further trouble and approach a curved bay. Thickly wooded hills run right down to the water's edge, a thin band of buildings fight for space between the sea and the forest. There's no quay, so the boats have found an unusual way of mooring, anchoring out in the bay and taking a long rope from the stern to the shore so that they line up neatly like cars in a car park rather than swinging freely on the anchor chain. I've never seen it before, but it strikes me as an extremely efficient use of space.

'We'll need to get the line to shore. Shall I swim with it?' I ask. Before Dad answers, a dark-haired man in a grey cotton shirt and cropped trousers pops his head up next us. He's standing up in his rowing boat, holding onto the side of *The Alcina*.

'Welcome to Trebizond,' he says with a broad smile. 'I take line for you.'

'That would be very helpful,' Dad says, giving him the end of the rope and a few coins to say thanks. We find a space between two boats wide enough for *The Alcina* and manoeuvre our way in. The man rows towards the shore, letting out the rope bit by bit as he goes. He hops ashore and ties the end to a rusty iron ring bolted to the pavement. From the deck, Dad gives him the thumbs up. We check the anchor is firmly in, aware this next stage of the journey will take weeks, maybe months.

We gather the essentials: sleeping mats, water bottles, as much food as we can carry. I add my fire starter kit and penknife. Aria slings her bow and quiver of arrows over her shoulder. Pippin emerges from her cabin with two bulging backpacks. She puts one on her back, and the other across her tummy, making her waddle like a duck.

Aria frowns. 'Do you really need so much—' A furry head pokes out.

Pippin scratches Hobnob under the chin. 'He's coming with us. There's no way I'm leaving him on the boat. He's been alone for too long.'

As we close *The Alcina* up, I get a lump in my throat. I swallow hard and hop off the boat, not trusting myself to look back.

The port is a collection of mismatched buildings packed tight together to create a noisy, bustling town. 'Hee-haw.' Over the din of the street, a donkey brays. People move out of the way as it strolls down the middle of the street. It has a brightly coloured cloth over its back and a wicker basket strapped to each side. Several long, thin loaves of bread stick out the top of the baskets. 'Do you think they're going for a picnic?' Pippin asks.

'That's just how they carry stuff,' Dad says. As the donkey passes, people pluck loaves out and toss coins in. 'Actually, I guess that's the bakery.' He laughs and gives us each a coin. 'There are a few market stalls over there, why don't you see if they've got honey ice?'

As we head to the market, a gaggle of children crowds round us. A question of whether other boats are coming startles me, but I look at the kid and see only innocence. I shake off the worry that he meant jet-ships. Standing slightly apart from the group, a young gypsy girl watches us. I catch her eyes. Old eyes, eyes that tell a thousand tales. She drops her gaze. Sunlight bounces off the band of tiny silver bells that trim her headscarf. They jangle as she melts into the crowd.

With much arm waving, Dad explains to a group of locals that we're actually headed straight to the train station. The crowd laughs. 'Ha ha, a train. You'll be waiting a long time,' a man says. 'Would you like room? I have very nice guest room. Clean. Good price, special discount just for you.'

A woman scolds him. 'Leave him be, I'm sure the train will arrive soon. It's only a couple of days late.'

'This week, no train. I sure of it. Shall I take you to see the room?'

Another man joins the group. He slaps Dad heartily on the back. 'Ignore them. You're in luck, I just heard the train is on its way. You'd better get along to the station sharpish though or you won't get a seat. Follow me.' He herds us through the crowd. More than once I'm sure I hear the tinkling of tiny bells but the little gypsy girl is not there.

At the far end of the street, the road runs into the train track and the pavement turns into the platform, bustling with activity: rumours of a train have spread fast. A screech announces its approach. Clouds of steam pour from the chimney as it chuffs towards us. The brakes squeal when it pulls alongside the platform and it grinds to a halt in a hiss of steam. Passengers surge out, carrying bundles of clothes, small children, and chickens in equal quantities. Steaming corn cobs and fragrant rice parcelled up in giant, green leaves tempt us as we try to board the train. Aria buys a few, handing over a six-sided silver coin.

'Don't forget to get something for Hobnob,' Pippin says.

'What do you think he'd like?'

'Fish.'

'Fish.' 'Fish.' 'Fish.' The vendors pass the request back through the crowd. A few seconds later, a grimy hand holds up a fat fish.

'Perfect.' Aria takes it, thrusting a coin into the waiting hand.

Pippin sniffs it and wrinkles her nose. 'Pooh, I don't think that's very fresh, but I guess Hobnob won't mind.'

We clamber up into the train. The carriage is filled with rows of hard, wooden benches which remind me of church pews. Metal racks above our heads overflow with luggage. Small children bounce on knees, while chickens peck on the floor. A bleat from beneath one of the seats makes Hobnob's ears prick up and he wriggles free from the backpack and darts under the bench. Pippin squeals and crawls after him. The passengers let out great big belly laughs at the chaos. Eventually, Pippin persuades Hobnob to stop chasing the other animals and, once he's safely back in his nest, everyone shuffles along the already packed benches magically creating space for us. A man yanks the window down, letting some fresh air into the stuffy, over-crowded carriage.

With a loud whistle, the train pulls out of the station in a cloud of steam. We slip left and right on the polished wooden seats, it's just as well we're packed in like sardines in a tin or we'd slide right off the benches. A heady aroma fills the carriage as Aria hands each of us a hot corn cob and a parcel of rice. She offers the leftovers to our neighbours to broad smiles. '*Teşekkür ederim*,' they say. Pippin breaks a few chunks off the fish and feeds Hobnob. More smiles, despite the pungent fishy pong. The corn cobs and rice parcels have been reduced to husks and wrappings. People settle down for the long journey and start to talk amongst themselves. We're soon forgotten.

Pippin hangs out of the train window, her eyes wide with excitement. 'Hellooo,' she cries to a group of children walking beside the track, clutching schoolbooks. Everyone waves.

As we leave the town behind, the tracks slice through well-tended fields. Stream trails from the chimney at the front of the train. Every so often, the driver sounds the whistle to alert villagers using the train track ahead as a makeshift road and they pull their mules over to the side. After a few hours, the chatter dies down. Despite the hard and uncomfortable bench, I doze off.

Peals of laughter from under my seat wake me up. I peer underneath. It's Pippin and a baby goat. I knew I heard something bleating. 'He's eating my shoelace,' she squeals, pointing at it chomping away happily.

A lady wrapped in brightly coloured woven blankets, a sleeping baby nestled in a sling across her chest, rubs the goat on the nose, 'Oh let go, silly billy. Hang on, I'll find your toy.' She pulls a battered leather shoe out of a fold in the blankets and waggles it in front of the goat. With another bleat, it spits out Pippin's shoelace and latches onto the tastier treat. Pippin wriggles back into a gap on the bench and re-ties her soggy shoelace. For a second, through the chuff chuff chuff of the train, I'm sure I hear the jingle of tiny bells. I check over my shoulder for the strange gypsy girl, but she's nowhere to be seen. I must have imagined it.

The train judders to a halt. Passengers automatically start to gather their belongings. Someone opens the carriage door and they spill out onto the dusty ground.

'Why's everyone getting out here?' Pippin asks, staring out of the window.

'Border control,' Aria says. 'We'll walk through immigration, then we'll all get back on the train again.'

The border consists of two high fences, topped with coils of barbed wire, separated by about twenty metres of no-man's-land. Grim-faced soldiers patrol each side, machine guns slung over their shoulders, rows of dull silver bullets wrapped around their waists. A guard opens a gate in the fence, scowling at us as we file through. In a straggly line, we trudge across the scarred, war-torn landscape; picking our way over the charred, blackened soil pitted by bomb craters, past the hulk of a burnt-out tank, past the piles of rubble and litter. Litter everywhere, blowing in the wind. All the time, the guards watch us through empty eyes. On the other side, we form a line by a desk under a rough wooden shelter with a small brass plaque proclaiming, "Immigration". An official in a sand coloured uniform takes a seat, flanked by two heavily armed guards. One by one we're ushered forwards to present our papers. A young man is dragged to the side and left on a bench, his head bowed. Although he clasps his hands, it doesn't hide the shaking. Conscious of our assumed identities, my knees knock as my turn comes and I stumble, landing in the dust. Nobody helps me up. I reach the desk and hold out my papers. The official glares at me until my eyes sink to the ground, then he scrutinises every page. My heart pounds as, sloth-like, he reaches for the ink stamp. Finally, he thumps my papers with a heavy black stamp and tosses them back without a smile.

Once we're all through security, our train is shunted onto another track. The young man is dragged to his feet and thrown onto the train, then, with a puff of steam, and only one passenger on board, it sets off back down the track we arrived on. Nobody blinks as it disappears into the distance;

they spread blankets onto the hard, dusty ground in the shade of a few scattered trees and settle down in small groups.

'Where's the train gone, Dad?' Aria asks. 'I thought we got back on once we were through the border.'

'I thought it was a direct train,' Dad admits, as we plonk ourselves under a small, scrubby tree. 'I guess another train will be along soon enough.'

Daylight fades and even the other passengers are getting fidgety. Pippin rolls around in the dust playing with her new best friend, the baby goat, giggling as it nibbles her fingers. Several passengers unroll sleeping mats, resigning themselves to a long wait. Some distance away from the group, a young girl spreads out a heavily embroidered piece of fabric on the dust and kneels in the middle of it. As she pushes back her hood, exposing a headscarf and a fringe of tiny bells, I see those eyes. The gypsy girl.

ELEVEN

GYPSY

She must have been on the train with us all the time. Annoyed I hadn't spotted her, I march over. 'Are you following us? What do you want?'

'There are stories that need to be told.' Her voice tinkles like the bells on her headscarf. 'A story for you. A story for them.' She gestures towards Aria and Pippin. 'A story for everyone. The only question is where they begin and where they end. Would you like to hear your story? Or …' She frowns. 'Or maybe you already know it.'

'Please, tell me my story,' I beg.

She picks up a bundle of well-worn tarot cards with gilt edges, each one the size of a postcard, and fans them out. 'Pick one.'

My hand hovers over the deck. The back of each card is richly decorated with an intricate swirling pattern of reds and greens, purples and blues. I reach for a card but at the very last second change my mind and tap the one next it.

She plucks it out, glancing at it before sliding it back into the deck. 'It is as I thought.'

'Wait,' I cry. 'Can't I see it?'

She shakes her head.

Anger surges through me. 'Why not? If it's my story, why can't you tell me.'

'Your story is already well told. Do not ask again. Now it is the turn of your sister.'

'Humph. I'll ask if she wants to, although I'm not sure there's much point if you don't say anything.'

I stomp back to my family and pull Aria to the side. 'See that gypsy girl? She says she'll do you a tarot reading, if you can be bothered. Mine was lame.'

Aria nods. 'I think I should. Come with me though.' She walks over, with me close on her heels.

'Sit.'

Aria sits cross-legged on the cloth. I plant my feet and fold my arms across my chest. This time the gypsy spreads the cards, face down, on the cloth.

'Choose.'

Aria points at a card. In silence, the gypsy studies it then, keeping it close to her chest, tells Aria to pick another, then another. Five cards in all before the gypsy raises a hand to signal *Stop*.

The gypsy returns the cards to the pack and shuffles them. 'Wait, can't I see them? What are they?' Aria cries.

'No need for you to see them, they were crystal clear: *At the monastery lies what you seek, but not until the sky-island will your quest be complete*. Does that make sense?'

Aria turns to face me. 'What we seek? That must be the relic. It's in a monastery. That must be where the star is pointing. But what's a sky-island?'

'Never heard of it before,' I say.

'Do you know?' Aria asks the gypsy.

She shrugs. 'Sorry, you'll have to figure that out yourself.'

Pippin pops up next to my elbow, hopping up and down, 'My turn, my turn.' The gypsy waggles a finger at Pippin, a gesture that seems far too grown-up for her years.

Pippin takes Aria's place on the cloth and points at five cards. The gypsy gathers them up. Her brow furrows as she studies them, and she squints at Pippin. 'Curious.' She sweeps the cards up, shuffles them, and lays them out again.

Pippin touches five new cards. The gypsy's eyes flicker as she picks the cards up. This time she lays them face up in front of us. The first four show the familiar pirffu, hyrshu, kasai, and eagha charms. The final card has a picture of identical twins, an explosion of silver sparks coming from where their fingertips touch.

'Well, I know about the charms, but who are they?' Pippin asks, pointing at the twins.

The gypsy leans forward and presses her thumb to Pippin's forehead, her eyes glazing over.

'Well? What does it mean?' Pippin prompts her.

The gypsy blinks. She holds out the tarot card with the twins on it to Pippin. 'A gift for you.'

Pippin shakes her head. 'I can't take that. You need it. I mean, your deck will be incomplete without it, won't it? You won't be able to do any readings?'

'These cards have been in my family for many centuries. When they pass to the new generation, you learn all the stories. All the stories except for one. This one. Nobody has ever drawn this card. Yet you drew it not just once, but twice. Curse, blessing, or promise, please, you must take it.'

Pippin hesitates before taking the card and tucking it into her backpack. With that, the gypsy pushes the remaining cards into a pile in the middle of the cloth and ties them in a bundle. She stands up. 'These stories have been told. Now they've been given life, they no longer need me to carry them. But other stories still wait.' She turns and walks away into the empty landscape. As the light fades, her tinkling voice floats back, 'Find the monastery.' I watch until she's just a speck on the horizon. Not once does she glance back.

TWELVE

SPLIT

It becomes obvious we're here for the night and everyone settles down to sleep. Dawn is announced by a loud screech which makes everyone leap up as a steam train comes into view. We watch its progress as it puffs and pants towards us. We scramble into the carriages and sort ourselves back onto more wooden benches, nodding and smiling at our travel companions. The train creeps along the track, so slow that at times it feels like it's barely moving at all. The journey is interrupted by frequent stops where a gaggle of engineers spill out to make adjustments then we creak back into action. The passengers shake their heads and tut and grumble. Several of the smaller children cry constantly, their parents unable to soothe them to sleep as the train jolts and judders. The hours drag by. Day turns to night and we try to sleep, jostled and shaken. I wonder if keeping your eyes closed counts as sleep. I do some maths: if twenty minutes of keeping your eyes closed was equivalent to two minutes of actual sleep, how much sleep have I had. My body tells me the answer is none.

The last stop is announced by a whistle. We hang out of the windows to see where we are. Ahead of us, the train track peters out in a small village, no more than a single road with ramshackle buildings scattered on either side. Cattle and goats wander freely. A group of barefoot children kick a ball on a dusty football pitch. Beyond the village, the snow-capped Himalayan mountains rise into the clouds. From here on, we're on foot.

'Can we still reach the monastery before deep winter?' Aria asks.

'Hopefully,' Dad says. 'The high roads will be buried under thick snow and black ice already. Some of the lower mountain passes should still be open.'

'What do the monks do when the roads are closed? Are they completely cut off for the whole winter?'

'They're pretty much self-sufficient. Once the roads are closed, nobody goes up or down. Even if the roads are still open, we might not find any local guides willing to go with us until spring. We can't risk the journey without a guide,' Dad says. 'That would be suicide. Especially in winter.'

'But we can't wait until next spring. Sir Waldred and Morgan will beat us to the relic.'

'Then we'll have to hope we find a guide, but first, we need provisions. We should be able to barter for fresh goats' milk and eggs from farmers on the way, but this is the last proper chance to stock up.'

We cram the provisions into backpacks and sling them over our shoulders. I sag under the weight, but it's only temporary so I don't complain. Soon enough, I'll be scraping around in the bottom to find a few crumbs. Then we're off; the final stage of the journey is underway. There's a bounce in my step as we follow the dirt track out of the village towards the foothills. Pippin starts to sing, *'It's a long way …'* Aria joins in, each as tuneless as the other. I stick my fingers in my ears in an attempt to block out the racket, which only encourages them to crank the volume up. As soon as they finish one song, they launch into another, on and on they go, however, as the hours pass and the sun beats down relentlessly, Aria lapses into silence, until I can only hear a faint hum from Pippin, and eventually even she falls quiet. There's no bounce left in any of us, just a hot, hungry, tired, trudge.

When the sun is high, we find a scrap of shade from a spindly tree and collapse. It's hard to believe we'll be knee-deep in snow in just a few days' time. Aria tears a loaf of bread into chunks and passes them round before producing a huge, round cheese wrapped in a red-checked cloth. I dig out my pen knife and cut slices for everyone. I swig a few mouthfuls of water from my flask. It's warm; functional but not the refreshing ice-cold blast my body craves. Lunch finished, we doze, waiting for the heat of the day to ease off. After a while, Dad stands up and stretches his arms above his head. The others start to gather their kit up. I squeeze my eyes tight shut, reluctant to move. Dad prods me with his foot. 'Come on, lazybones. Another ten miles today.' With a groan I drag myself upright.

Several hours later, we pass a village; a scruffy cluster of wooden huts perched on stilts with goats, chickens, and pigs penned underneath.

'Is there a mountain guide here?' Dad asks one of the villagers, miming walking and pointing up the mountains.

The villager frowns and shakes his head. We hoist the backpacks onto our shoulders and set off again.

Every time, we get the same response. No. No. No. We're running out of villages and we still don't have a guide. We trudge on. The sun sinks beneath the horizon and the temperature plummets.

I wake before sunrise to the sound of a kettle whistling. Aria's perched on a log in front of a small fire. The promise of hot tea tempts me to move. Wrapped in a blanket, I tiptoe towards her, careful not to wake Dad and Pippin. She shuffles along to make space. I rub my hands together and hold them out to the fire.

It's not long before the others wake up and, as soon as we've drunk our tea, Dad is keen to get going. It's too cold to sit around, anyway.

Today the distances between the villages are far greater. With each one we pass through, the chances of finding a guide diminish. As we approach a few scattered huts, not enough to be called a village, Dad pauses. 'This is it,' he says. 'The very last village. It's now or never.' He approaches a group of villagers digging in a field. We don't need to hear the conversation; the head shaking tells us all we need to know. He comes back to us, 'It's no good. There are no guides this late in the year. We'll have to turn back.'

Aria scratches her head. 'Don't give up yet, there might still be a way.' She points to a small paddock where several mountain ponies, their winter coats already thick and shaggy, are grazing. 'Even though we don't have a guide, I wonder if they'd sell us those ponies? If the journey was quicker, and easier, maybe we could still get through the mountain passes before the big snow,' she says.

There's a derelict looking hut beside the paddock. Aria climbs up to the first floor and taps on the door. A slender girl of about fifteen opens it, blinking in the bright daylight. Her dark hair stands up in short, uneven, spikes, pushed back from her face by a brightly patterned bandana. She's wearing a blue cotton shirt with the sleeves rolled up, and loose-fitting grey trousers, cinched in tight with a piece of rope. Stout leather boots are laced up to her shins. She puts her hands on her hips.

'Hello. We were wondering, are any of your ponies for sale?' Aria asks. She points at the ponies and waves a thick wodge of notes: the universal language of cold, hard cash.

A scowl flashes across the girl's face and her eyes darken, but in a blink, it's gone and she's laughing. 'Why would you want that ragged bunch of ponies?' she says, in flawless English.

Aria smiles at her. 'You speak English! We're trekking up into the mountains. Ponies would be such a big help.'

'I can't sell them.'

Aria's shoulders sag.

The girl continues, 'But you can borrow them. We need them back to plough the fields in the spring.'

The girl clambers down the steps. As we head for the paddock, the ponies trot straight over to the gate. A fat skewbald, its coat covered in big brown and cream splodges, nuzzles Aria. She scratches it behind the ear.

The girl hesitates, a faint sweat breaking out on her forehead. 'I must warn you …' She wipes her brow.

'Warn us about what?' Aria prompts.

'Nothing. Just watch the weather,' she mumbles. 'By the way, that's Purli. He's very lazy.' The girl bites her lip and studies us. 'Where's your guide?'

'We haven't got one,' Dad says.

'Not surprised. Winter is coming. It's madness to go now. Snow has already closed the highest mountain passes. Spring would be a much better time to go.'

'We can't wait,' Aria says.

A spark flashes in the girl's eyes. 'Why not? What's so urgent? Where are you going?'

Aria ignores the first two questions and waves her hands in the direction of the mountains. 'To the monastery,' she says.

'The monastery doesn't take visitors,' the girl says, frowning, 'and you don't look like students. Why are you in such a rush to get there?'

'We have to … find something,' Aria says.

'I shall be your guide,' the girl announces.

'You? What about the farm?' Dad asks.

'There's not much to do here in the winter other than to look after the hens and my brother can do that.'

'Well, if you're sure. That would be fantastic,' Dad says. 'We really do need a guide. It's too easy to get lost up in the mountains, especially if the weather turns bad. What's your name?'

'Nele.'

We introduce ourselves, omitting details like me being a Sea-Tamer, or Aria being an Air-Rider. While the girls chat, I pull Dad aside. 'There's a problem. There aren't enough ponies for all of us.

'I know. I'd been thinking we should split up. I could go back and check on Mum. I trust you and Aria, and I know you'll both look after Pippin.'

The girl flinches. *Was she eavesdropping?* I look sideways at her, but her face is a mask.

Dad continues, 'Anyway, my long legs would trail on the ground if I rode one of those ponies. It really wouldn't be fair to make them carry me, so that's sorted then.'

Now the numbers work, the girl allocates us ponies.

'You'll like Razcal,' she says to Pippin, bringing a toffee coloured dun pony with big, soft, chocolate-brown eyes over to her.

'Rascal? Is he naughty?'

'It's Ra-Z-cal. He's good as gold. Don't worry about him. He won't put a foot, or hoof, wrong.'

She gives Aria the lazy skewbald. 'You've already made friends with Purli, so that's easy.'

Next, she puts a head collar on a cappuccino coloured palomino with a cream mane and tail. It pins its ears back and bares its teeth. I take a step back. 'It's OK,' she says, holding the lead rope out to me. 'This is Yetchr. He's actually quite friendly when you get to know him, and I reckon he's the best pony we have. He's really brave, and fast, and his canter is as smooth as butter. If you don't fall in love with him when you start riding, I'll swap with you. Promise.'

She goes up to the last pony, a bright chestnut mare, the colour of a ginger-nut biscuit, and scratches her withers before popping the head collar on. 'I'll take Doli.'

Yetchr refuses to stand still while I groom him. He paws the ground and swings his body away from me. Then, when I try to pick out his hooves, he plants his feet firmly on the ground and refuses to budge. Clearly, I'm going to have to prove myself worthy before we bond.

Nele brings the tack out from the hut. Heavy, western style saddles, with a big pommel, a fluffy sheepskin covered seat, and chunky leather stirrups. Perfect for long days in the saddle. She swings the first one up onto Doli's back. I pick up Yetchr's saddle and attempt to copy her motion. It weighs a ton. The saddle lands with a thump on his back. Yetchr shoots me a look that says "Amateur" and Aria stifles a laugh as she flicks her saddle up. Nele helps Pippin with her saddle then shows us how to tighten the girths and attach saddle bags stuffed with water bottles and provisions. Pippin holds up Hobnob. 'What about him? He needs to come too.' I lash Pippin's backpack to her saddle, making sure Hobnob is snug as a bug inside it.

Dad gives each of us a big hug before helping us mount up.

Nele half turns her back to us, but I see her rip a blank sheet of paper from a notebook and scribble something on it. She rolls it up tight and uses a bit of leather cord to tie it to the fence. 'What are you doing?'

'Just a note to … my err … brother. I thought I should tell him where we're going,' Nele mumbles. Then she sets off across the plains for the foothills. Twisting round in the saddle, I wave over my shoulder at Dad, standing alone in front of the hut.

THIRTEEN

HUNTED

The ground is perfect for riding; not too hard, not too soft. Some areas are cultivated, and we go around them, not wanting to destroy any of the precious crops. Food is scarce enough in these hard times. When the land opens out, we let the ponies enjoy long fast gallops. Yetchr is always far out in the lead. We've established a mutual respect and he's every bit as amazing as Nele promised. I'm going to be very sad when I have to say bye to him at the end of the trek. Razcal and Doli trot along happily; two of the easiest, best natured ponies I've ever encountered. Purli dawdles behind the others. He's not a speed machine like Yetchr, but he's solid as a rock. As we approach the foothills, we drop the pace, riding with long loose reins allowing the ponies to stretch.

'Where did you learn to speak English?' Aria asks Nele.

'Did a bit of freelance work last summer,' she mumbles.

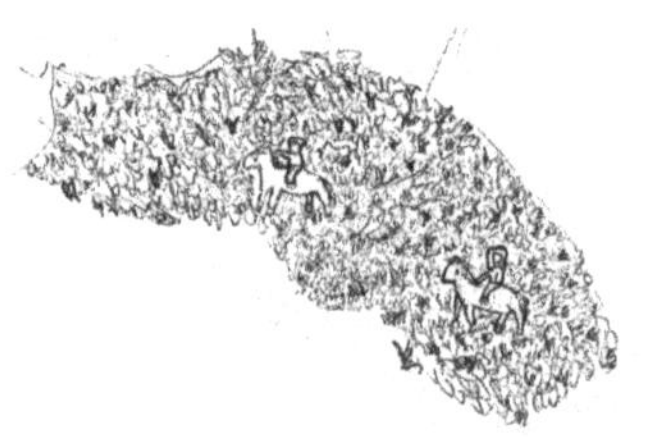

'What kind of work?' Aria asks, but Nele kicks Doli sharply in the ribs and gallops off without answering.

After several hours, we stop for a rest. Nele wipes the sweat off the ponies' flanks. Far behind us, across the wide, flat grassy plain we just crossed, clouds of dust swirl into the blue sky. The acrid smell of smoke drifts in the wind and a faint rumble fills the air. It gets louder. Engines. That can only mean one thing: bounty hunters, heading straight towards us.

'How did they find us?' Pippin cries.

Aria leaps on Purli, bareback. 'Hide. I'll draw them away.' She urges Purli forward into a gallop, whooping and waving her arms above her head like a Zulu warrior. Ears flicking, nostrils flared, and eyes wide, the fear gives Purli extra speed and his hooves fly over the ground. 'Wait for me, I'll be back,' she shouts over her shoulder.

I scan the plain for a hiding spot. Not too far away from us, a rocky outcrop juts out from the long grass. Scant cover, but better than nothing. We certainly can't stay out here in the open. I whistle at Yetchr. He lifts his head and trots over to me, Razcal and Doli tag along after him.

We slip halters on and lead them over to the rocks. They're poorly hidden, I hope their coats blend into the scenery from a distance. Nele offers to hold the ponies while Pippin and I check what's happening. Her hands shake as she takes the reins, and she chews her lip.

We worm our way up the biggest boulder on our bellies, knees scraping along the rough stone. 'They've taken the bait and gone after Aria. I don't think they saw us,' I say.

From our look-out, we watch the mud-bikes gain on Aria. I kick myself, Purli's so much slower than Yetchr, I should have gone. She can't outrun them. The bikes split up, trying to trap her. I spot her plan and nudge Pippin. 'She's going to jump the river. There's no way they'll be able to follow her.'

'It's too wide. She won't make it,' Pippin says.

Purli leaps into the stream sending a huge splash into the air. He stumbles, going down onto his left knee, but regains his balance. Aria urges him forward. Deeper and deeper. Then he's swimming. Aria clings onto his mane. Behind them, the bikers skid to a halt by the edge of the river. There's no bridge out here on the plains. They're stuck. Angry voices reach us as they shout first at Aria, then turn on each other. The current pushes Purli swiftly downstream but he keeps on swimming. Then he's on his feet again, pushing his way up onto the other riverbank. As soon as they're out of the water, Aria leans over his left shoulder to check his leg for injuries from the stumble, but he must be fine as she breaks into a canter and he isn't limping.

One of the bounty hunters shakes his fist at Aria as she gallops away. 'We'll get you later,' he shouts, then in a cloud of dust and smoke, the bikes spin round. *Are they coming for us now?* Pippin and I slide down the rock and take the lead ropes for our ponies from Nele, shortening them, ready to leap on, but the thunderous growl of the bikes gets fainter. Relief floods through me and my body sags against the rock. We crawl back up and watch the trail of dust disappear along the riverbank. I turn to Pippin. 'They'll try to ford the river further down. We're safe here, for now. We can wait for Aria to come back. Keep an ear out for engines just in case.'

The sun is high in the sky when I hear hooves. Pippin springs to her feet, but I yank her back down into the long grass. 'What if it's not Aria,' I hiss.

'Who else could it be?' she says, wriggling free. She jumps up and down, waving her arms wildly. 'Aria, we're here. You did it!'

Aria trots over. 'Purli did it, really,' she says, patting him. 'He's such a star.' She gives him a hug and slips from his back. 'He might not be the fastest pony, but there's no doubt about his bravery.'

We tack up and set off again, leaving the flat plains and heading into the foothills. Cushioned with moss, the mountain path winds its way up through a forest of fir trees. All day, we climb steadily. By dusk we've left the gentle foothills behind and the ground gets harder. Sure-footed, the ponies cross the frequent streams and loose scree slopes without stumbling.

As the light fades, we stop to set up camp. Without a word, Nele untacks the ponies, checks them for injuries, and picks the stones out of their hooves. Aria grabs her bow and arrow and heads into the scrubby woods to find something for supper. Hobnob stalks off into the undergrowth. Just a few paces in, he hunkers down, his tail swishing this way and that. He pauses then raises his body a fraction and slinks forward, inching closer to his prey. Then he pounces. *That's one dinner sorted,* I think.

I lead the ponies over to the stream. Yetchr demands my attention, stomping his hooves in the water like a kid playing in the waves at the beach. Only once I'm soaked to the skin does he stop. Back in camp, I tie them loosely to bendy tree branches so they can munch on the grass. It's best they eat their fill now as the grass will get sparser the higher up the mountain we go.

Pippin emerges backwards from a thicket, dragging what appears to be an entire dead tree. I make a circle of stones for a fire pit, build a little teepee shape out of twigs, and dig out my fire starter kit. Sparks fly from the flint stick onto the silver birch bark shreds and it's not long before the fire splutters to life.

Night falls and there's no sign of Aria. My stomach rumbles. When she finally returns, a couple of mountain hares slung over her shoulder, I leap up and dance round her, whooping for joy. Once they're skinned and gutted, we use twigs as skewers and roast them over the crackling fire, picking pieces of steaming meat off with our fingers.

Bellies full, exhaustion takes over. The fire flares as we pile all the remaining branches on top and settle down in a circle for the night. I'm not sure how long I'm asleep for, but I wake to find Hobnob sitting on my chest, prodding my face with his paw as if he's trying to wake me up. Nele's empty bed catches my eye. I hear a faint rustle and the thin sliver of moon casts a weak shadow. It's Nele. She checks over her shoulder then raises her hands to the sky. I lean over and shake Aria gently. She sits up, rubbing her eyes.

'Shh, don't move. Nele's up to something,' I say, pointing to the shadowy movement. Hobnob lets out a soft miaow, but in the dead of night it's as loud as a foghorn. Nele lowers her arms and walks back towards us.

'Are you OK?' Aria asks when she returns to camp.

'Just … err … stretching my legs, I couldn't sleep. Hope I didn't wake you, sorry.' She lies down on her sleeping mat and turns her back on us.

Aria looks at me and mouths, 'That was weird.'

FOURTEEN

BETRAYED

The thick moss makes a soft mattress and I sleep deeply, waking only when Aria wafts a mug of strong, sweet, black tea under my nose. Pippin and Nele sit wrapped in blankets beside the fire embers, clutching their drinks. Cold air nips at my fingers and the tip of my nose is bright red.

'We need provisions before we go any higher,' Nele announces as we breakfast on the last of our dried fruit and nuts. 'How are you at foraging? Can you tell the difference between edible mushrooms, and poisonous ones?'

'Of course,' Pippin says. 'And I can recognise wild herbs too.'

'Great. The three of us will go foraging while Aria hunts,' Nele says. 'Let's meet back here in a couple of hours. We won't be going anywhere today.'

'We could hike after we've been foraging, there will still be a good few hours before nightfall,' I say, but Nele shakes her head.

'No. We will not be trekking today. Today, we will gather provisions and rest. Camp will be here again tonight.'

She knows we're in a rush, so I don't understand why we're wasting a day. I frown, puzzled by her reluctance to move, and turn to Aria. 'Don't you think we should press on?'

Aria shrugs. 'She's the guide. The journey is about to become much tougher and I suppose it might be wise to have a day of rest before we tackle the next stage.'

We split up to forage and meet a few hours later back at camp. Nele spreads out our haul on a cloth on the ground, discarding several of my more colourful mushrooms. 'That should last us several days,' she says.

Aria nods. 'Since we're hanging around here, we might as well use the time to preserve the meat. Finn, could you build us a smoker, please?'

I dig a hole and lay the fire at the bottom while Aria skins the hares. Pippin crushes some herbs with a stone and spreads the paste onto the strips of meat before hanging them on a rack made of sticks in my improvised smoker. We cover the top of the hole with branches to keep the smoke in. Once they're dried, they'll keep for ages so we can pack them for the journey. The mushrooms and rest of the herbs are tied into neat bundles and stowed in our saddle bags.

Next morning, we pour water on the fire and scatter the cooled ashes. The meat in the smoker has dried into thin strips. I take a bite. It's tough and leathery, and takes ages to chew, but tasty. I wrap the strips in a piece of rabbit skin. We groom and tack up the ponies and set off for another day on the trail.

After a while, the ground trembles and a familiar rumble fills the air. Bounty hunters. I knew we should have kept moving yesterday. Hearts in our mouths, we dismount and pull the ponies off the path into the fir trees. The branches flex as we push through but spring back into shape creating a thick screen. The engines get louder. Yetchr is restless, prancing on the spot. I scratch him behind his ears, and he neighs. Flashes of sunlight glinting on metal are visible through the trees as they get closer. We freeze. Nele chews her fingernails. Yetchr paws the ground and whinnies. One of the bikers slows down and looks around. He cuts his engine and takes off his helmet, rubbing his forehead with the back of a leather-gloved hand.

'Did you see something?' another calls back.

He peers into the trees, then shakes his head. 'I don't think so.' He shoves the helmet back on and roars off after the others.

Once the engine noise has faded away, we lead the ponies out of the trees and back onto the path. Yetchr fidgets, his ears flicking backwards and forwards constantly, while Purli snorts like a steam train.

'I wonder how they found us?' I say, thinking aloud.

Nele stares at the ground. 'I'm going to walk the ponies in hand until they relax,' she says. She takes Purli from Aria and holds out her hand for my reins. As I pass Yetchr's reins to her, I catch her eye. She looks away.

'It was you,' I gasp. 'You betrayed us. You led the trackers to us. That's why you wanted us to hang around yesterday. It was nothing to do with rest, it was to give them time to catch up. How did they know where to find us?'

She hangs her head and mumbles, 'I sent a messenger-bird.'

I picture her in the moonlight, arms raised. She must have just released the bird into the air at that point. 'Why would you do that to us?'

'I didn't want to. They made me promise to tell them about any visitors to the monastery. They threatened to burn our crops if I didn't. My family would starve. I'm sorry.' She grabs

Doli's mane and leaps on. She looks back over her shoulder at me. 'Get away from here. They'll be back.' With a hard kick in the belly, Doli breaks into a canter.

'Poor girl,' Aria says, watching Nele disappear down the track. 'Imagine being threatened like that. I reckon they've forced her to work for them before. It would explain her excellent English, and she did rather avoid the question about how she learnt it.'

'I'm sorry for her too,' I say. 'But right now, I'm more worried how much she told the bounty hunters. They know we're going to the monastery. Just as well she didn't know about the relic.'

Pippin blushes and her hand flies to her mouth. 'Oh no,' she says. 'I sort of told her.'

I grab her by the shoulders. 'You did what? How could you do something so stupid?'

Pippin averts her eyes. 'She kept pushing me. Asking again and again why we were going to the monastery.'

'But we'd agreed not to tell anyone.'

'It seems obvious now that she was a spy, but I thought she was on our side. I've put us all in danger, haven't I?'

I take a deep breath and count to ten, letting my arms drop to the side. 'I'm sorry, I shouldn't have got cross with you. She tricked us all. How much did you tell her?'

Pippin holds her head in her hands. 'I just said it was a mystery and we had to go to the monastery to solve it.'

Aria sighs. 'Ah well, we can expect to meet Sir Waldred at the monastery then.'

'It doesn't really change anything. We're not in any more danger than we were before, Sir Waldred was always going to find out about the monastery sooner or later ...'

'I'd rather it was later, much later, like after we've found the relic and gone home.'

'Me too, but we are where we are. The question is, what do we do now we've lost our guide? Should we go back and try again in spring?'

Aria grabs me. 'No. It's a race against Sir Waldred now. I know it's dangerous, but we must keep going. If we stay off the path for the next couple of days and keep an eye out for the bounty hunters, we should be OK. Luckily, they make so much noise we'll hear them long before we see them.'

Progress is much slower off the track as we're forced to loop round obstacle after obstacle: boggy patches, fallen trees, and impenetrable thickets. Nightfall brings a sharp bite to the air. Winter is coming. Grim and silent, we set up camp. I spread our blankets over the ponies, securing them with bands of fabric stretched over the backs and tied under their bellies. Aria and Pippin build us a small shelter using sticks balanced between two trees, padding it with leaves and moss. It's just big enough for the three of us to wriggle underneath. Hobnob curls into a ball on top of Pippin's toes, like a hot-water bottle.

When I wake, Aria is pacing up and down in front of our shelter, rubbing her hands in the frosty morning air. Pippin's fast asleep. I edge my way out of the shelter carefully so as not to disturb her. Snowflakes are sprinkled over the ground. Winter arrived overnight.

Aria and I have finished our meagre breakfast by the time Pippin crawls out of the shelter, her eyes still full of sleep and bits of twig stuck in her hair. While she grabs a rusk to munch on, I clear all traces of our stay, scattering the sticks from our shelter widely and using a branch to wipe our footprints away. I pull Aria aside. 'We need to go faster if we're to stand any chance of crossing the mountains before the snow makes them impassable. What do you think about going back to the track?' My breath comes out in clouds.

Aria nods. 'I'd been thinking the same.'

Back on the path, we climb rapidly, but the higher we get, the harder it snows. A flurry of snowflakes at first, then so thick and fast our vision is blurred, and the world turns grey. When we stop for lunch, I clear the snow from a patch of grass for the ponies to graze on.

Clumps of snow gather under the ponies' hooves. Yetchr slips and stumbles. 'We'll have to walk,' Aria says, dismounting. 'It's not safe to ride like this.'

I pull a tub from my saddle bag. 'It's just an idea, but I think I know why Nele packed this.' I open the tub and scoop out a dollop of grease with my fingers, smearing it thickly onto Yetchr's hooves. 'This should stop the snow from sticking.' We take a few paces, it works.

Snow falls hard and fast, burying the trail under a thick white blanket. I can barely see my hand in front of my face. Dangerously easy to get lost in this.

FIFTEEN

MONASTERY

Onwards and upwards we trudge through ever-deeper snow drifts. The first glimpse of the monastery takes my breath away. Carved directly out of the mountain, six white, marble towers disappear into the clouds. A solitary snow eagle circles high above it. The path twists as we make the ascent. Eventually, we turn the final corner and the footpath leads to a wide archway. The ponies are on edge, twisting and turning, as we approach. We dismount and walk beside them, arms draped across their necks to reassure them there's nothing to fear. They stare at us with wide, trusting, eyes.

Icicle spikes hang down from the arch, sharp as barbed wire. I snap one off as we pass under and suck it like a popsicle. I wince at the bitter taste and toss it onto the ground.

A monk, covered from head to toe in pristine white robes, appears from the shadows and intercepts us. His thin robes fly in the wind and, despite the snow, he's wearing sandals. From under the hood, comes a voice. 'I was expecting … a girl.'

'Hello,' I say. His shrouded head flicks in my direction then he turns his back on me.

A second monk appears. I smile at him, but his face is blank. Without uttering a word, he takes the reins from our hands and whisks the ponies away.

'Wait, where are you taking them?' I call after him. He doesn't even glance round.

The white monk answers on his behalf, 'To the stables, of course. It is warm, and there is food and water for them. They must rest after their long journey.' Something about his voice nags at me.

I move to follow Yetchr, but he blocks my path.

'Let them be. Come, we must go this way.'

Fresh snow crunches underfoot as we step into a hexagonal courtyard. Tall, thin, silver birch trees and perfectly manicured bonsai trees, their trunks twisted and contorted, fill the space. Flowers droop under the weight of large, white petals. I pull one towards me and sniff it, expecting to be hit by a heady fragrance, but there's nothing. Disappointed, I let it ping back. A shower of petals flutter to the ground. We pass a few monks tending the garden; they pay us no attention, as if we're invisible.

The white monk turns into a covered walkway supported by slender marble pillars. An icy wind whips through the space sending a chill deep into my bones. He gestures towards a chamber. Hobnob jumps as if he's had an electric shock, his fur standing on end, then scoots up the nearest tree.

'It's OK, Hobnob,' Pippin says. 'There's nothing to worry about here. It's a monastery. We couldn't be safer. Come on down.' He doesn't budge. 'Do you want me to come and get you?' She jumps up and down trying to catch the lowest branches, before collapsing in a sweaty heap.

Aria clutches her stomach laughing. 'You look like a jack-in-the-box. Just leave him. He'll be fine. He'll come down when he's ready.'

Pippin calls up the tree, 'Stay there then if you want, but you won't catch any mice, so you'll have to come down sooner or later.'

'Hurry up, we have much to talk about,' the white monk commands, a sharp note catching in his voice.

Aria steps through the huge wooden door, followed by Pippin. I move to follow them, but the monk blocks the doorway. He places his hand on my chest. 'This conversation is not for you.'

'But ...' I protest.

The white monk shakes his head. Peering out from behind him, Aria nods at me. 'It's OK. We'll be fine.' The wind catches his hood, lifting it a fraction, and I see him glaring at me. They say the eyes are the window to the soul. His are black as night. He tugs the hood back over his face and slams the door shut. A bolt clanks into place.

'Aria, wait. I don't trust him. Let me in.' I fling myself against the door, but it doesn't budge. I promised Dad I'd look after them. I slump to the ground, my back against one of the ice-cold, marble pillars. There's no point sitting here feeling sorry for myself. With a sigh, I drag myself to my feet and return to the courtyard.

On the far side, I spot another chamber, the door flung wide open. I tiptoe towards it, but the gardening monks are so oblivious to my presence I could probably sing at the top of my voice and they still wouldn't notice. I peek inside. Glass cabinets stretch from floor to ceiling. Ceramic jars line the shelves, each one decorated with a delicate blue design and a brass name plate on a chain hanging round its neck. A young monk sits on a bench, frowning as he makes detailed notes in an oversized book. He's probably about my age, but it's hard to judge.

I take a deep breath and step through the doorway. 'Hello, I'm Finn.'

The boy jumps in surprise. At least that means I'm not invisible.

'Hi. I'm Rahfi,' he says, with a shy smile. 'What are you doing here? Nobody ever visits us, not in winter anyway. Although the monks were expecting a visitor.'

'Well, they seemed very pleased to see the girls, not so much me.'

Rahfi places his quill in a groove at the top of the desk, leans back, and links his fingers. 'Girls plural? That confuses things. Do they have wings?'

'Wings? No, of course they don't.'

'That's a shame. The monks were expecting the winged girl from the prophecy to arrive soon. Girls without wings will be most disappointing. Maybe she'll arrive tomorrow.' He picks up his quill and focuses on his work again.

I open my mouth to tell him that he's being far too literal in his interpretation of the prophecy. Aria doesn't need wings to fly, but my nerves are still jangling from the glare of the monk and my gut is telling me to be careful who I trust, so I bite my tongue and change the topic. 'What are you writing?'

'Research notes. I'm studying to be an apothecary.'

I peer over his shoulder at the page. "*Gangliforme*" it announces, double underlined. Two-thirds of the page is covered by the most detailed drawing of the human body I've ever seen. Each vein and organ meticulously drawn in black ink and neatly labelled. Rahfi closes the book and pushes it away. He yawns and stretches his arms above his head. 'I've been at it for hours and could really do with a break. Do you want me to show you around the temple? Have you seen the Great Library yet?'

'Nobody has shown me anything. I'd love a tour while we wait for the girls to come back.'

'Cool.' Rahfi opens a closet in the corner of the room where a number of identical robes hang. He thumbs through them, selecting the most faded, worn-out looking one. 'You stick out like a sore thumb dressed like that. Put this on, it's my old robe so it should fit you. Much better to blend in, I always find. We'll get fewer questions, and the fewer questions people ask, the easier life is. Strictly speaking, I shouldn't be in the Great Library without the permission of a senior monk. Not until I finish my training.'

I take off my jacket, shivering in the chilly air, and pull the thin cotton robe over my head. It's too short and my boots stick out the bottom. Rahfi rummages around in the bottom of the closet and produces a pair of sandals.

'You have to be kidding, my feet'll freeze in those.'

He tosses the sandals at me and holds his hand out for my boots, stashing them in the closet along with my jacket. 'Right, let's go.' He stops in front of a pair of carved wooden doors, at least three times my height. Rahfi turns the handle and slips inside, yanking me through the gap after him. Inside, the library is long and thin. A soft yellow light filters through the high windows. Alcoves line both sides of the central aisle. Above each entrance swings a brightly painted wooden sign: history, geography, chemistry, magic, physics. The central aisle bustles with monks coming and going, all carrying stacks of books and manuscripts. Large, saffron-yellow cushions are scattered randomly on the floor; groups of monks sit cross-legged, reading.

My jaw drops as I take in the sheer scale of the library. I've never seen so many books in one place. Since books were banned by the Earth Lords, most of the great libraries were burnt to the ground. The few that remain are kept in secret in what I had previously thought of as libraries but, compared to this, were nothing more than a few bookcases hidden away in a cellar, like our collection on the boat. 'Wow. How come you've got so many books? Why haven't the Earth Lords destroyed the library?'

'As I said, we don't get many visitors, so I guess not many of them know. And it's not exactly easy to get here, so even if they do know, they usually can't be bothered to make the trip, preferring to pretend they don't know. Those who do come would secretly admit that, occasionally, it can be useful to check something in a book.'

So, the Earth Lords have visited here in the past. I shudder at the thought. 'Well it's pretty cool. I'm glad you showed me.'

'Wait until you see the heart of the library. That's where we're going. It's the best bit.' Rahfi tugs me behind a bookcase. 'Here, take these. It'll make us look more inconspicuous.' He thrusts a towering pile of books into my arms and gathers another for himself. 'Follow me.' The ease with which he navigates his way round as we dart in and out of alcoves, dodging the monks, suggests this rule breaking is a pretty regular occurrence.

About halfway along the hall, he dumps his pile of books on the floor of an alcove. We flatten ourselves against the bookshelves as a monk goes past. Rahfi sticks his head out and looks right and left. 'Coast's clear,' he says, tugging my sleeve. 'Look.' He points at the floor. The tiles are laid out in the shape of a heart, an intricate design etched into it. The pirrfu charm, the mark of a Sea-Tamer, around my neck starts to beat like a heart, ba-dum … ba-dum … ba-dum. It gets louder and faster. More urgent. Ba-dum-ba-dum-ba-dum. I try to focus on the design in the tiles.

Rahfi continues, 'They say if you spin round three times, then spit on the heart, you're guaranteed to come back here one day. Try it.' He pushes me into the middle of the heart, grabs my shoulders and spins me round.

Badumbadumbadum. Round and round. Dizzy. Feel dizzy. Stagger. Going to be sick. Round and round. BADUMBADUMBADUM. The charm. Last time it did this … then it all goes black.

SIXTEEN

CAVERN

I open my eyes. The heartbeat from the pirrfu charm is a steady ba-dum, ba-dum, ba-dum. I'm flat on my back in the far corner of an alcove, the arched ceiling of the Great Library soaring high above me. The tiled floor feels cold through the thin robe. Rahfi kneels beside me. He prods me in the ribs. 'Are you OK?'

I push myself up. 'Ouch. Yes. I'm fine. Stop prodding me, please. What happened?'

'You fainted. I dragged you back here. Are you sure you're OK? Should I get one of the monks?'

'I'm OK. How long was I out for?'

'Not long, only a few seconds, but you were mumbling. Utter nonsense. You bumped your head quite hard. Clearly affected your brain.'

'Someone was talking to me. They were telling me something really important.' I scratch my head. 'What was it though? I can't remember.'

'It sounded like you were saying, "It's all gloop". Sorry, told you it was nonsense.'

The conversation comes flooding back to me. 'Algol. Not all gloop. I need to find something called Algol. There must be a book about it in here.'

'Never heard of Algol. But if we start in the archives, they might have a record of it.'

'Fine. Where are the archives kept then?'

'Uhm, over there.' He waves his arm vaguely.

'Show me.' We stick our necks out of the alcove and he points at some rose-wood filing cabinets in the busiest part of the library. Monks buzz to and fro constantly. Grateful for my disguise, we sneak over to the cabinets. Rahfi starts flicking through the cards, muttering, 'Alghero … Aldigus Mons … Algiers … Algoa Bay. Here it is,' he says. He waves an index card under my nose, grinning from ear to ear. 'Told you I'd find something. ALG-978-201. It's a star. Should be easy enough to find.' He hurries over to the far side of the library.

As we pass the astrology section, I tug his sleeve. 'Surely, it's in there?'

He shakes his head. 'Wrong index numbers.' He dashes this way and that, checking the shelves, the search increasingly erratic. 'This can't be right. I can't find it. The reference number doesn't make sense,' he grumbles.

My heart sinks. 'Are you sure we're looking in the right place?'

Rahfi shows me the index card. 'This is definitely right ... oh no.' The colour drains from his face. 'There's a sub-code ... -DEM. *Amitabha, Amitabha, Amitabha*,' he murmurs a prayer.

'What's wrong?'

'That classification is only given to D ... D ...' he stutters, his voice failing.

'Demons.' I finish the word for him. I sigh, it *would* be in that section. It could have been faeries, or mermaids. But no, that would be far too easy. It's a demon. As if I didn't have enough on my plate already. 'It's not fair,' I grumble. 'I can't see what a demon has to do with me.'

'The universe has a way of showing us what we need to know. All life, and death, is connected. Anyway, the books on demons aren't kept here. They're in the—' He lowers his voice to a whisper. '—in the Shrouded Crypt.' Rahfi points to a dark corner of the library. 'But you don't want to go there, trust me. That's a very bad idea. It's too dangerous. Not even the most senior monks dare to read those books.'

'Why bother to keep them then?'

'Knowledge. The monks seek knowledge. But knowledge of demons is dangerous. The more you learn, the more exposed you are. One monk thought he could study demonology a few years ago. He vanished. I don't think anyone has been into the crypt since then.'

I pull my shoulders back, I don't have a choice. 'Even so, I need to go in. Please could you show me?'

Rahfi sighs. 'I'll show you, but I'm not setting foot inside. Not even a toe.'

At the back of the library, a narrow spiral staircase winds its way down into the gloom. A wooden sign swings over the entrance to the Shrouded Crypt. Written in sharp black letters on a pale wooden board is a single word. Demonology. A shiver runs down my spine. Rahfi picks up a candle in a brass chamberstick with a handle and gives it to me. 'Aren't you going to help me find it?' I call over my shoulder.

Rahfi makes another quick prayer. 'I knew this would happen. Look, I'll come in and get it for you. But I'm not staying around if you plan on reading it.'

Twelve steps down and we're in the crypt. Compared to the rest of the library, it's dusty and ill-lit, with a sharp chill in the air. Twelve bookcases line the walls. I shiver.

'The monk who vanished ... only his pipe was ever found, lying there, on the floor.' Rahfi points at a spot towards the back of the crypt. A dark red stain marks the tiles.

The books are packed tightly together. Brittle leather book covers in blood-red, forest-green, and brown so dark it's almost black. Burnished gold letters embossed into the spines. 'So, where's the book on Algol?' I ask.

Rahfi runs his finger along the shelves, counting them off. He stops. He's standing right on top of the bloodstain, but I don't think he's noticed. I don't point it out. 'This is it,' he says. 'But I really don't think you should touch it ...'

Algol: a study on the infinite nature of demonology is etched into the spine. I tug it from the shelf. Across the cover, the words *"DO NOT OPEN"* have been scratched. The cold has numbed my fingers and, as I struggle to prise the pages apart, it slips from my hands. It hits the floor, falling open as it lands. Around it, the floor starts to dissolve. We edge back, deeper into the crypt, but the hole grows and grows until it reaches our toes and still it doesn't stop. Rahfi screams and drops the chamberstick, plunging us into darkness. Beneath our feet, the ground crumbles and we tumble into a black abyss.

I land with a bump. I wriggle my fingers and toes. Good, nothing broken. 'Rahfi, are you ok?'

'Not really,' says a voice in the gloom. 'I've had better days. Told you it was a bad idea. Now look what's happened. We've fallen into a hole. Oh, and don't forget we probably just set a demon free. Because, even though the book said very clearly, in big letters that even an idiot could read, "*Do not open*", you went and opened it. And I can't see a thing. I really hate the dark.'

'Hang on.' I open my backpack and take out a small torch. The dim yellow light illuminates the chamber. I shine the beam upwards, just in time to see the hole in the library floor far above our heads close with a *pop*. I sweep the beam of the torch to my left and right. The book lies a few feet away from me. I crawl over and pick it up. I try to open it, but the pages are sealed tight again. With a scowl, I hurl it against the wall.

Rahfi looks around. 'I think I preferred it when it was dark. Now I can see where we are. At the bottom of a pit with no way out. Brilliant. Just brilliant.'

'There's a tunnel,' I say, forcing my voice to sound bright and optimistic.

'Oh goodie. Let's go and have a look. I'm sure that will be loads of fun.'

The tunnel heads down. Deeper and deeper. It must be an Earth-Wanderer construction, nobody else would dig so deep. Claustrophobia grips me as the earth presses in. I force myself to breathe. Tall candles, their bases thickened by rivers of ancient wax, are crammed into notches in the wall. One after another, they spark to life as we pass, lit by an unseen hand. I turn the torch off to save the batteries and shove it into my backpack. Eventually, we emerge

into a circular cavern lit by dozens of flickering yellow candles. Stone tablets covered with an ancient script line the walls. My fingers trace the intricate carvings.

'Rahfi, can you read these?'

He squints at the writing. 'Course I can. It's Sanskrit. Most of the old manuscripts in the monastery are written in it. I always thought it was a bit of a waste of time learning it, but I guess not. Where do I start though? There must be over a hundred tablets in here.'

'Good question. Let's just work round the room. Can you see if they mention anything about Algol? After all, that's what brought us here.'

'Nothing on this one,' he says, moving onto the next tablet. 'Nor this one.' He's halfway round the cavern before he stops. I hurry over to join him.

'And? Did you find something? What does it say?'

'It's a bit complicated. I'd better read it to you …'

"May the pirrfu, hyrshu, kasai, and eagha charms bind this demon-goddess Algol to her celestial form and banish her to a place beyond the skies. Only but once a year, may she return to Earth for the chance to repent before a gathering of clan elders. If all agree to her plea, then may she be rebirthed to a physical form."

Rahfi studies the inscriptions while I search around the rest of the cavern.

There's a scratching noise. Rats? No. I spin round. Scanning the chamber, I realise the it's coming from over to my right. I follow the noise, coming to a halt in front of a tablet. Halfway down the tablet, the writing stops. As I stare at it, there's a loud scratch and a line appears in the stone, then another scratch and a squiggle appears. I spin round to check the other tablets: before this one, they're all covered with writing; after this one, they're all blank. History is being written as we watch.

'Rahfi, you need to see this.'

Rahfi clenches his fists as he translates the emerging words. 'The banishment hasn't worked. She's out there, committing new crimes. How is that even possible? She was only allowed on Earth for one day a year for the gathering ...'

'There can't have been a gathering in centuries, not since the clans went into hiding, so, if she came for a gathering, it hasn't happened. Which means she's still here. Waiting.'

As if the walls had been listening, the scratching stops and the chamber fills with a deathly silence. Rahfi draws himself upright. 'If I'm ever going to qualify as a monk, I can't allow a demon to roam the earth. Clearly, there isn't going to be a gathering any time soon, so it's up to me to find another way to banish her.'

'I'll help.'

'Help?' he snorts. 'Could you just start by getting us out of here? After all, it's your fault we're stuck in an underground cavern. Or maybe I'm actually dead and this is the underworld. That would really ruin my chances of becoming a monk.'

'Don't be silly. We're not dead. And we're not trapped either. Did you notice that some of the candles are practically brand new? Someone's been here recently, and there's no pile of skeletons in the corner, so it figures there must be a way out. We'll find it. No point going back down the tunnel, we know that's a dead-end.'

Rahfi groans. 'Oh well, there must be a secret door then.'

'Good idea. Let's check the walls.'

'You do realise I was being sarcastic, don't you?'

I ignore him and start to walk round the chamber, running my fingers round the edges of each tablet, checking for anything that might be a latch for a secret door. Rahfi plonks himself down on the floor, cross-legged.

'Rahfi, what are you sitting on?'

'Stone. Cold, hard stone. I'm imagining a nice comfy cushion though. And a pot of jasmine tea.'

'No, I mean, look at what you're sitting on. There's a pattern on the tiles. It's a heart, exactly like the one in the library.'

Rahfi leaps up and starts to spin round on his heels on it, like he made me do in the centre of the library just before I blacked out. The candles splutter and I'm plunged into darkness. Then, they spark back to life, and I'm alone. Rahfi's vanished.

I walk over to the heart pattern and put one foot on it. 'Here goes …' I mutter to myself and slowly start to spin round and round. Everything goes dark.

SEVENTEEN

ESCAPE

When I open my eyes, I'm back in the library. Flat on my back, on top of the tiled heart pattern. A headache hammers at the back of my eyeballs and even the soft yellow light of the library hurts. Rahfi is sprawled on the floor next me. His eyes are tight shut. I nudge him. 'Are you dead?'

'No, I'm not dead. Although hanging out with you is definitely not good for my health.' His eyes open a fraction. 'Hey, we're in the library. Told you there was a myth that if you spun round three times on the heart, it guaranteed you would come back here one day. I always assumed it meant for a visit, a bit of a holiday. Not that it would open some kind of magical transportation portal.'

I get up, my arms outstretched for balance as I still feel dizzy. 'Come on, Rahfi, stop chattering. We need to find Aria and tell her about Algol.'

We slip out of the library unnoticed. Back in the courtyard, the door to the chamber where the white monk took the girls is ajar, but the chamber is empty. Rahfi looks at me and frowns. 'Are you sure this is the right chamber? We don't use this room. Bad air. The monks don't like it. Who was she with?'

'I didn't ask his name, but it's definitely the chamber the white monk took her. He wasn't exactly chatty. Maybe one of the monks in the garden saw where they went. Let's ask them.'

The monks smile as we approach. One of them shuffles forwards and clasps my hand. They're happy to chat to us, but none of them saw us arrive.

'How could you not have seen us?' I ask. 'We were standing right here. One of you came out to greet us. And another monk took our ponies to the stables …'

'I fear you have been tricked. We are not quite ourselves today. Several of us feel we err … misplaced … some time earlier today'

'Misplaced?'

'Yes, as in, one minute it was early morning, then the next minute the sun was high in the sky, yet we had no recollection of the passing of time, as if we'd been in some kind of trance. We treasure every precious minute of life, so it was a bit odd.'

A trance would explain the blank expressions on their faces when we arrived. 'Who greeted us then?' I ask.

'I fear they were no monks, and there's only one person who would dare to impersonate us. Only one person who would dare to put a spell over us …' He lowers his voice to a whisper. 'Sir Waldred.'

'No, that's impossible. I would have recognised him …' Even as I say it, I realise my mistake. Two soulless black eyes haunt me. I know those eyes. And the voice. I kick myself for not realising sooner. 'He's got Aria and Pippin,' I cry.

The monks start to chatter. 'A girl? The winged girl?'

Rahfi puts his hand up. 'Don't get too excited. It's not her. She doesn't have wings.'

A collective sigh rises from the monks.

Now I feel bad that I didn't tell Rahfi the full story earlier. 'Sorry, I should have explained earlier, Rahfi, she doesn't need wings to fly. She just … kind of … walks on the air.'

The monks start to babble.

'The prophecy is true.'

'A blood-born Air-Rider here.'

'I never thought I'd see the day.'

I interrupt. 'Stop! Didn't you hear me? Sir Waldred has taken them prisoner. We've no time to lose. We need to rescue them.'

A heavy silence falls over the room. The monks look at each other and shake their heads. 'It's too late,' they say. One by one, the monks leave, 'Wait,' I cry, clasping the arm of the last remaining monk. 'We can't give up on them. It's not too late.'

'We do not give up,' a monk says, patting my arm softly. 'We merely restore our bodies with some precious sleep. Everything will be clearer in the morning. It always is.' With that, he guides me into a cell-like room, and closes the door behind me. 'Sleep well.'

If they won't help me look for the girls, I'll go on my own. I march to the door and twist the handle. Locked. I'm locked in. I'm a prisoner. Rahfi's not my friend. He's my captor. The far wall has a tiny window, I stand on tiptoes, but can't see out of it. I jump up and down a few times but only catch glimpses of the night sky. There's no way out, I'm trapped.

I pace up and down. Apart from a plain stone bed running down one wall, the room is empty. On the bed is a thin mattress and a neatly folded, scratchy-looking, grey woollen blanket. Compared to our camps on the trek, it looks like the most luxurious bed in the world. Eventually, exhausted, I stretch out on top of it, pull the blanket across my legs, and let my body succumb to the waves of tiredness.

Next thing I know, Rahfi is shaking me awake. He drags me through to breakfast. 'Hurry up, sleepyhead, this is the best meal of the day.' The long wooden tables in the refectory are already busy, even though the sun is yet to rise. The smell of freshly baked bread makes my mouth water. The monks tell me to help myself, and I don't need any encouragement, tucking into huge chunks of warm bread smothered in creamy goats' cheese until the skin over my belly is stretched tight, full to bursting. A wave of guilt passes over me. 'We should be looking for Pippin and Aria. I bet they aren't getting breakfast.'

'The monks have been searching for hours already. I said I'd bring you as soon as you'd finished breakfast.'

'Hours? The sun's not even up yet.'

'Since first prayers. I did come in to check on you, but you were so fast asleep I didn't want to wake you.'

Another wave of guilt washes over me for doubting the monks. 'So, where are they looking?'

'They started at the top of the monastery, in the towers, and are working their way down.'

I gaze up at the high towers. Then down at the ground. 'He's an Earth-Wanderer, we need to start underground,' I say.

'You want to go back to the c-cavern?' Rahfi stammers.

'No. There was other magic in there. He'd need somewhere which didn't affect his powers. Is there a cellar?'

Rahfi shakes his head. 'Monasteries rise to the skies, they don't go into the bowels of the earth.'

'Then where can he be?'

We sit in silence for a while. Rahfi absent-mindedly munches his way through another few chunks of bread, dipping them into a glass of goats' milk. He swigs the rest of the milk, licks his lips, and slams the glass down on the table. 'The well. It's the only thing here that goes down deep, and I mean deep. Really deep. I don't even think it has a bottom.'

I'm on my feet already. 'What are you waiting for then?'

Rahfi grabs the last of the bread and shoves it into his pocket then runs out the hall, with me close on his heels. We sprint through the corridors and into a courtyard. In the middle, is a well. A wooden bucket swings above it, bound together with three bands of iron. We peer down the well. It's brick lined, the bottom lost in darkness. I pick up a pebble and drop it in. I count to twenty before I hear a faint splash. 'There's water in it! They can't be down there. They'd drown.'

'Of course, there's water in it, it's a well. It wouldn't be any use if it didn't have water in it.'

'Hello?' I call. 'Aria? Pippin? Are you down there? Can you hear me?' My voice echoes into the darkness. Then I hear something, I hang over the edge, straining my ears. Something's down there. 'Quick, lower the bucket,' I cry.

Rahfi unwinds the end of the rope and cranks the wooden handle, lowering the bucket into the hole. Down and down it goes. 'The water's low after summer. We need the melt-snow soon.' Down and down, until it grinds to a halt. We've run out of rope. 'Now what?' he asks.

I hadn't thought about that. The bucket's far too small for anyone to climb into, even if they were down there. It was a stupid idea. I lean over and call out their names again. Silence. I sigh. 'Just bring it up, I guess.'

Rahfi starts to wind the long rope back up. I sit down, my back against the brickwork, my head in my hands. As Rahfi brings the bucket out, he squeals and lets go of the rope. The handle spins out of control and the bucket flies down into the depths. He grabs the handle to stop the free fall.

'What happened?'

'It hit something,' he says, winding as fast as he can.

I leap up and peer over the edge. The bucket comes into view, and I see a shape. It miaows at me. Hobnob! Poor thing. He must have fallen into the well. I console myself with rescuing Hobnob, even if we haven't found the girls. The bucket emerges into daylight and I reach in. I try to cradle him but he jumps out of my arms and shoots off.

'There's gratitude for you,' Rahfi says.

Hobnob darts back, winds himself around my legs, then scoots off again. The third time he does it, I realise he's trying to tell me something. He wants me to follow him. In leaps and bounds he runs through the archway and out of the monastery. Outside he turns in the direction they took the ponies. I look for their hoof prints, but they've long been covered up by fresh snow. I hope they're OK. After we find Aria and Pippin, the ponies are next on my to-do list. Hobnob stops by a section of wall covered with a thick ivy creeper. He scratches at the base, brushing a section of trailing ivy aside. Hidden behind it, I spot something wooden. I grab fistfuls of the green streamers and tear them down.

Rahfi's jaw drops. 'A secret door! Should we knock?'

'I don't think Sir Waldred will open it for us, whether or not we knock.' I drop to my knees and peer through the keyhole. It's pitch-dark inside. I stand up and turn the handle, unsurprised to discover it's locked.

From behind the door comes a voice. 'Finn? Is that you?'

I place my palms flat on the door. 'Aria, is Pippin with you? Are you both OK? Don't worry, we'll get you out of there.'

'It's locked.'

Rahfi snorts. 'You'd think the winged girl would be able to fly out or make an air-key or something cool.'

'Rahfi, that's really not helpful,' I snap. 'Who's master of keys in the monastery? Maybe you could go and find him?'

'Actually, I wonder if I could make an air key,' Aria calls. 'I've never tried before, but it might work.'

She goes quiet. After a few minutes I tap on the door. 'Aria?'

'Shut up. Stop distracting me. I'm concentrating.'

I pace up and down outside the door. 'Are you managing?'

'Give me a chance, Finn. It's not easy, you know. It keeps dissolving before I get it into the lock.'

I resume my pacing.

Finally, there's a click, the handle turns, and the girls stroll out. Aria beams from ear to ear. 'Turns out you can't keep an Air-Rider under lock and key. I don't think Sir Waldred will make that mistake again.'

'I can't believe that worked,' I cry, hugging her.

She laughs. 'If I'm honest, neither can I.'

Rahfi coughs. 'Uh-hum. Any chance of an introduction?' He gives a small bow to Aria then Pippin. 'Nice to meet you.' A chant soars from the temple. 'Bother, I'm late for prayers. See you later.' He darts off without waiting for a reply.

We follow him back into the monastery, chatting as we walk. 'What happened when you were with Sir Waldred?'

'He kept asking where the relic was. And saying that Morgan would deal with us.'

The name hits me. Morgan is my birth mother, but the clan elders forced her to put me into hiding when I was just a baby. She never forgave them and turned to Sir Waldred to get revenge. Even now, I can't believe she's evil.

While the monks are at prayers, I show Aria and Pippin the library. When we get to the tiled heart, I spin Aria round three times, just like Rahfi did to me.

'Stop it!' she squeals. 'You're making me dizzy.'

'It's a legend. You have to do it.'

'My turn,' Pippin cries, hopping from foot to foot.

Ritual completed, I take them to the Shrouded Crypt and point out the stain on the floor where the monk vanished. It's only then, as I start to explain about Algol, that I realise I left the book in the underground cavern after I lost my temper and threw it at the wall.

EIGHTEEN

RELIC

'We need to get back to the cavern, Aria. I need that book on Algol.'

Aria shakes her head, 'Finding the Air-Rider relic before Sir Waldred is our priority. Algol and the book can wait.'

She's right. 'So, the relic. Where should we start? The elder at Castle Gylen said we're looking for a glass feather. If you were a Guardian, where would you put it?'

'Up high, where Sir Waldred couldn't get it easily.' She tilts her face up to the painted monastery ceiling. 'Like up there. It could be disguised to look like it's part of the design. You could walk under it a million times without ever noticing.'

Aria casts a small whirlwind under her feet and rises into the air, wobbling slightly before finding her balance. She floats towards the ceiling and starts her search.

I call up to her, 'Use your hyrshu charm. I reckon it'll help you find it, like my pirrfu charm led me to the Sea-Tamer relic in the cave.'

She pulls the charm from under her shirt. It glints in the sunshine. 'I can hear singing.' Aria cries. 'It's coming from over there ...' The charm spins like a top as Aria hovers beneath a painting of a giant snow eagle. Another part of the prophecy makes sense now:

Where white eagles soar and no man can walk,
Above the clouds, yet still on the ground

Aria picks at the outstretched wing of the painted bird. Flakes of silvery paint drift down to the floor like confetti. 'It's here. I've found it,' she cries.

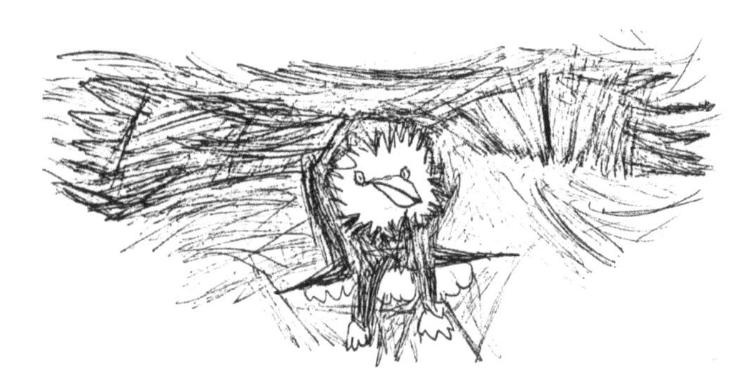

'Wait ... don't touch it. You need to put gloves on. Remember what happened when I touched the

Sea-Tamer relic? Sir Waldred saw me and sent the trackers …'

'I don't have any gloves,' she says.

'Here. You can use my prayer gloves,' Rahfi says, suddenly appearing at my side. I can't believe I hadn't heard him approach. I kick myself for being so careless. What if it had been Sir Waldred who'd crept up on us? I was too absorbed in the search for the relic, I must be alert at all times. Rahfi pulls a pair of white silk gloves from his tunic, bundles them together and tosses them into the air. Aria catches them with one hand and slips them on. She prises the feather from its painted bed and sinks back to earth with it cradled in her gloved hands.

Landing beside me, she opens her hands. There, resting on her palm, is the feather. It's smaller than I expected, and so delicate it looks like it would shatter with a single tap. 'We need to put it in the cube, but I can't open it.'

'You could make an–' Rahfi starts.

Aria interrupts. 'I already tried an air-key, but it doesn't work, the cube is protected.'

'Maybe they hid it in the painting with the feather?' Pippin suggests. Aria floats back up and starts to examine the vast ceiling, inch by inch.

'I don't think they'd keep them together,' I mutter. I turn to Rahfi. 'Where do the monks put things to keep them safe?'

'Under our seats in the temple. Each monk has his own seat, so nobody would ever find it accidentally.' He lowers his voice, 'It's where I keep my lychee gum.'

We leave Aria to check the ceiling and head to the temple in the heart of the monastery. An urn at the entrance is filled with incense sticks, to help carry the prayers to heaven. We pass between two huge statues. The first is of a familiar cross-legged Buddha, but the other is of a strange-looking being waving dozens of arms. Rahfi catches me staring at the statue. 'That's Avalokitesvara. He guides us on the path of compassion.'

Inside, the temple is richly decorated with gold leaf and crimson paint. High-backed wooden benches, divided by arm rests into people-sized segments, run down either side. Rahfi points out a narrow shelf, presumably intended for prayer books, tucked beneath the seats. He lowers himself onto his belly and wriggles beneath the first row. On the other side, I follow his lead. Almost every seat has something stashed away in the little shelf: a stack of letters, a well-thumbed book, a sapphire ring, a dried flower, a blob of chewed lychee gum – that must be Rahfi's seat.

'I can see you,' Rahfi calls. 'Don't eat my lychee gum.'

'Yeuch, no thanks, I wouldn't touch that.' I grimace and wriggle past.

A few seats further down, I spot a sky-blue silk pouch tied with a dark blue cord. It bulges slightly, there's something inside. My fingers fumble with the cord as I open it. A single silver key drops into my palm. I stand up, dusting myself off. 'Hey, Rahfi, I've found it. Or at least, I've found a tiny key, far too small for any door in the monastery, which looks like it might fit the cube. I'm going to take it to Aria.'

Rahfi wriggles out from the other side of the aisle.

Back in the hall, Aria is still searching the painted ceiling. Pippin is lying on her back on the floor shouting up a constant stream of random instructions, 'What about over there? Or there? Or that bit?'

'Shh, Pippin.' I say. She rolls onto her tummy and pulls a face at me. I ignore her and call up to Aria, 'Come down. We've found a key. Pretty sure it's what we're looking for. Let's try it.'

Aria drifts back to the ground, landing on her feet as light as a feather. She tugs the stone cube from her backpack.

Rahfi wrinkles his nose. 'What's that?'

'It's a kind of … relic translation device,' I say, struggling to think how best to explain what the cube does. 'If we put the relic inside it, we should be able to read any messages left by the Guardian. We used it once before with the Sea-Tamer relic and it showed us where we needed to take the relic to hand it over to the elders.'

'But we know where the elders are, so it might not have a message this time,' Aria adds. She tries the key in a few locks before we hear a tiny click and a compartment springs open. It's lined with the same sky-blue silk as the pouch that the key was in. Having used the cube before, we know how this works. Aria places the glass feather on its silken bed.

Pippin jumps up and down. 'Well? Can you see anything? Is there a message?'

Aria's eyes glaze over.

'And?' Pippin twists Aria round to face her waves her hand in front of her face. 'Aria?' She doesn't reply. 'I don't think she can hear us.'

Aria blinks and her eyes refocus. 'It was a message from the Guardian, but it wasn't about the relic. It's about a demon. The one you were talking about in the library, Finn. It's about Algol.'

I kick myself again for forgetting to bring the book with me from the cavern. 'What did they say?'

'Well, a lot of it was the same as what you'd already told me. But the Guardian claims she's escaped from the star-cell.'

Rahfi nods. 'Yeah, we figured that out. She came back for a gathering, but there can't have been one since the clans went into hiding. The clan elders didn't really think the terms of the banishment through particularly well, did they?'

'Sadly not. As loopholes go, they left her a really big one. But that wasn't all the Guardian said. Which do you want first – the good news or the bad news?'

'The good news. Definitely the good news. Let's just stop after the good news. Do we really need to have the bad news too?' Rahfi says.

Aria laughs. 'Afraid it doesn't work like that. The good news is, the Guardian thinks they know how to banish her back to the star-cell: if we can get her to the sky-island, the star will reclaim its prisoner.'

'Brilliant,' Rahfi says. 'Just brilliant. You call that good news? Persuade a demon to visit a sky-island from where they know they'll be transported back to their sky-cell. I'm sure Algol will just trot along happily for a spot of sightseeing, no problem. And you do realise that humans can't travel to the sky-islands, so how on earth are we supposed to get her there?'

An image of the little gypsy girl we met on the train journey pops into my head. Didn't she say that we needed to find the sky-island? Maybe she can help us.

Aria interrupts my thoughts. 'Air-Riders can get there,' she says.

'You can?' Rahfi's jaw drops. 'Can you really walk amongst the clouds? Have you been before? What's it like?'

'Technically I haven't yet, but the Guardian said I *could* go. I need to tell you the bad news though.

Algol offered Sir Waldred power beyond his wildest dreams. He couldn't resist the temptation.'

I snort. 'No surprise there. We already know he's a power-crazed megalomaniac. That's not new news.'

Aria ignores me and continues, 'That wasn't the bad news. There was … a price to pay. In return for the power, he gave her a gift. A body, a human body, to live in.'

'A body? Whose body? His?' I ask.

'No. Far worse than that.'

'Whose then?'

'You're not going to like this. Finn, he gave her Morgan's body.'

NINETEEN

DISCOVERY

'Morgan? My birth mother? Sir Waldred let a demon possess her?' I clench my fists and bite back my anger, counting to ten in my head before I speak. 'No wonder she betrayed the clans. I knew she wouldn't have done it on purpose. We have to find her and free her.'

'I bet she isn't far away,' Aria says.

'There's one guaranteed way to bring her here,' I say. 'Touch the relic.'

'Too risky. We can't battle Algol until we know how to defeat her.'

Too late. My un-gloved fingers reach out to the cube where the glass feather rests on the silk bed. The instant my fingertips brush against the relic, a jolt of electricity shoots up my arm. Smoke pours through the windows, long snake-like tendrils, twisting and coiling towards us.

'Finn, what have you done?' Aria cries, her face a mask of horror. She snatches the cube away from me. 'We're not ready.'

A clawed hand reaches out from the smoke and plucks the stone cube from Aria's hand. A tentacle of smoke snakes around her waist and flings her across the room. She lands in a crumpled heap. Aria springs up. 'Don't worry. I'm fine. Just a few scratches, but she got the cube. And the feather's inside!'

A high-pitched cackle echoes around the hall. I look up at the vaulted ceiling. Morgan. Not human, a monster, hanging upside down from a beam twenty metres up in the air. The demon Algol. She waves the feather, taunting us.

'It's mine now, all mine.' She screeches, diving out of a window.

Aria springs into the air. In a single bound, she flies through the window, landing with a thud on the red roof. Tiles shatter beneath her feet, tumbling to the ground and smashing into a million pieces. We run outside to watch. High above us, Algol vaults over a chimney, with Aria hot on her heels. Halfway across, Aria's foot crashes through the rooftop. She catches the edge of the crumbling roof and pulls herself back upright. Around her, the roof collapses, a gaping hole spreading by the second. Aria breaks into a run, staying just inches ahead of the growing hole. Algol leaps across the gap to the next building. Behind her, Aria grinds to a halt, teetering on the edge of the roof. From the ground, she looks tiny. Rahfi claps his hand over his mouth.

'Jump,' I cry. 'You can do it. Don't look down.'

Aria takes a few steps back and runs towards the gap. I hold my breath. The gap suddenly looks three times as big. As she jumps, I squeeze my eyes shut.

Rahfi grips my arm. 'She's not going to make it,' he cries.

I open one eye and will her on. She lands in a crouch like a cat on the next building. I let my breath out. They sprint towards the bell-tower. Algol pushes past the great iron bell. She turns and swings it hard to block Aria's path. It starts to chime. Bong, bong, bong. The monks in the courtyard look up, confused. Still Algol runs on, bounding from building to building across the monastery, faster and faster. But Aria's gaining on her. Confidence growing, her leaps get longer and longer, swallowing five then ten metres at a time. Just as she's about to catch Algol, the demon stops and turns to face her pursuer.

With a cackle, Algol tosses the feather into the air. As it tumbles towards the ground, she laughs, 'Ha ha. I destroyed your magic; I destroyed your magic.' The sky fills with a thunderous rumble. The ground quakes and Sir Waldred rises up through the earth on a cloud of dust. He grabs Algol and drags her underground. With a puff, the ground closes over their heads, and a final cackle echoes around the monastery.

Bewildered, the monks stare at the spot where Sir Waldred and Algol vanished. There's no time to think about them though. The feather spins through the air. Rahfi and I sprint towards it. From the rooftop, Aria casts a jet of wind, but misses. I call on my powers. Nothing. I try again. Still nothing. This far from the sea, I'm powerless. Aria takes another shot. The rush of air bumps the feather, sending it into an even faster spin. It twists and turns towards the ground. Suddenly, the earth starts to tremble again. The heavy marble paving slabs splinter and crack.

'Look out! Sir Waldred's coming back,' Aria screams.

A cloud of dirt shoots up into the air, swirling round and round. It sucks the feather into the vortex, smothering it, obscuring it from sight. Then the twister shrinks back into the ground. It's too late, it's gone. We lost the relic. But as the dust settles in a thick layer on the ground, there's something resting on a pillow of dust. It sparkles in the sunlight. The feather.

Quick as a flash, Aria grabs it and blows the dirt off. 'It's undamaged,' she cries, clasping it to her heart. She looks around. 'But where's Sir Waldred? I thought he'd come back for it.'

'Me too. I don't understand. Why didn't he let it smash into pieces on the floor?' I spot Rahfi, lying flat on his back, staring blankly at his hands. His mouth hangs open. 'Rahfi, it was you. You did that. That was magic …'

'My hands feel funny, but I swear I didn't do anything. One minute I was thinking about protecting the feather from smashing, then the next minute the earth just exploded in front of me. I thought Sir Waldred was back.'

'That's what we all thought. But he isn't. That means it wasn't his magic, it was someone else's. An Earth-Wanderer. And since it's not me or Aria, it must be you.'

Pippin puts her hands on her hips. 'What about me? I could have done that,' she says.

I grin at her. 'Sure, of course you could. I meant it must be either Rahfi or Pippin. Was it you, Pippin?'

She looks at the ground. 'No, but it could have been. I *can* do stuff.'

'So, can we agree it was Rahfi?'

Pippin sticks her bottom lip out. 'S'pose so.'

'Rahfi, who are you?'

'Nobody. Just a trainee monk. My parents left me on the monastery doorstep, wrapped up in a bundle of rags, with a scribbled note saying, *My name is Rahfi. Please look after me*, tucked into the folds. I don't even know their names. The monks have taken care of me ever since. Never even had a visit from my parents. I guess they really didn't want me.'

Aria turns to me. 'That sounds very like what happened to you, Finn, doesn't it?'

'Just what I was thinking. Rahfi, my parents also gave me up when I was a baby. But it wasn't because they didn't want me. The clan elders forced them to hide me, in order to protect the blood-magic. After that display, I'm pretty sure you've got the blood-magic too. I bet your parents were forced to hide you.'

Rahfi drops to his knees and rests his forehead on the floor in a prayer position.

Aria rushes over to him. 'Are you OK?'

He sits up, his face white as a sheet. 'Not really. This makes no sense. I'm not special. For a start, there's no prophecy about me.'

'There isn't a prophecy about me either,' I explain. 'But it doesn't change the fact that I'm definitely a Sea-Tamer. Aria's definitely an Air-Rider. And now it seems you're an Earth-Wanderer.'

'It's impossible. I've met Sir Waldred loads of times. Surely he'd have recognised me.'

'Maybe not. How old are you?' I ask.

'Eleven and a half.'

'Well you shouldn't get your powers until you're twelve. I doubt he'd have been able to sense anything before then, even if you were standing right next to him. But Aria's powers arrived early, not long after I got mine, and now yours have too … Aria, you're bleeding …'

'Am I?' She looks down, and her face goes pale. A puddle of blood stains the white marble floor. On her leg is a deep gash, she must have cut it when she fell through the roof tiles. I rip a section of fabric from the bottom of my shirt and tie it around the wound. The blood seeps through the fabric and, it makes me think. Three blood-magic children. Three Relic Hunters. It's as if the blood-magic is drawing us together.

TWENTY

PORTAL

'Do you think Sir Waldred knows the relic wasn't destroyed?' I ask Aria.

'Not yet, but it won't take him long. We'd better deliver the relic to the elders as soon as possible.'

'How? We're stuck here until spring. There's too much snow now, and no food for the ponies.'

Aria slumps. 'We're sitting ducks here. Sir Waldred could reappear at any point. I know it's dangerous to leave in deep winter, but it's also dangerous to stay here. We could take a sledge and load it with enough food. Maybe even a warm tent? It wouldn't be too heavy …'

Rahfi clears his throat. 'Uh-hum. I have a funny feeling … an idea … You know how the hearts connect the library and the cavern. Well, I'm pretty sure I've seen that symbol in some of the old explorer maps. What if they're all connected? If we can find where the other hearts are, maybe we can travel between them? What do you think?'

'It's worth a try,' I say. Aria nods.

'Let's go back to the library. I can get permission for us to study the maps, so we won't have to sneak in. The exploration studies teacher is a friend.'

As we enter the Exploration alcove, the monk's face crinkles into a huge smile. 'Young Rahfi, I'm inordinately pleased your studies have led you here. The world is too big for you not to look beyond the monastery walls. How can I help you and your friends voyage far and wide today?'

'We're interested in this symbol,' Rahfi says, sketching the heart shape on a scrap of parchment. 'Have you ever seen it on a map?'

The monk scratches his head and a frown crosses his face for a second, then he smiles again. 'Now that's an interesting symbol. May I ask, what is your purpose in studying it?'

Rahfi shrugs. 'I feel drawn to it.'

'As good a reason as any, and I'm glad you didn't use a false pretence. Of course, you already know about the one that is marked here in the monastery, but I never understood why it was included in the map. The symbols are supposed to show features: cliffs, mountains, valleys, lakes. It makes no sense to mark a piece of decorative tiling. But you're right, there are others. Let me see if I can locate them.' He shuffles off, then turns back, 'Come on, what are you waiting for? I'm not going to do all the work for you. You're quite old enough to help.' Not wanting to seem lazy or ungrateful, we hurry after him.

He moves surprisingly quickly between the shelves, pulling a map from here, another from there, and another, and another, until the three of us are staggering behind him entirely unable to see over our towering piles of paper. Finally, he stops. 'That should keep you busy for a while.' He points to the far corner of the alcove. 'Those desks are free this afternoon. You may use them. I will make sure nobody disturbs your studies.'

We dump the mountain of maps onto the desks and pull up four chairs. 'Where do we start?'

'Well, we need to take the relic to Castle Gylen, so let's start by looking for maps of the Northern Lands. Hopefully we can find a heart nearby.'

It takes several hours to sift through the maps but we locate about a dozen heart symbols in total and narrow it down to the two that are closest to Castle Gylen: one in the Outer Isles and the other over on the Emerald Isle. While we're debating the best option, a gong sounds.

'I can't believe the time! The library is closing for evening prayers. We'll have to pack up and come back tomorrow,' Rahfi says, starting to fold away the maps and stack them into a neat pile.

'Can't we just take the maps with us?'

Rahfi looks horrified. 'No, the books must not leave the library.'

'But we can bring them back tomorrow,' I protest.

Rahfi gives me a withering look. 'You've already lost one book from our library.' A chant rises from the temple and Rahfi dashes out. 'I'm late for prayers again, can you finish tidying up? See you at supper.'

I slip the two maps into my backpack, but Aria stops me, 'Leave them here. Let's take a break and come back fresh tomorrow.'

Reluctuantly, I tip them out of my backpack and Aria puts them back on the pile. 'Right, let's see if there's anyone in the dining hall,' she says. Of course, it's empty when we arrive, the monks are all at prayers. We take our places at the end of one of the benches to wait.

After prayers, the monks file in. Rahfi bounds across the hall and slides along the bench to sit next us. He grabs a slice of bread and starts to cram it into his mouth. 'My stomach would not stop rumbling all the way through prayers. How am I supposed to achieve enlightenment when I'm starving,' he says, with his mouth full.

Daylight streams through the tiny window in my cell. I stretch, surprised again by how well I slept on such a rock-hard bed. I run a hand through my hair in an attempt to tame the curls. A bowl of cold water and a clean, neatly folded rag sit in the corner of the room. I scrub my face and hands and even have a go at the back of my neck. When I squeeze out the cloth, the water turns grey. I feel refreshed and ready for the day. There's a spring in my step as I leave the cell to join the others.

Back outside the library, the first rays of sunshine have yet to take the chill from the air. We stamp our feet to keep warm. A look of surprise crosses the librarian's face as he opens the heavy wooden door and finds us queuing outside. We head straight to the Exploration section and toss our bags under the desks. Aria spreads out the maps on the table in front of us. 'Votes?'

'The people of the Outer Isles have a fearsome reputation as warriors. I doubt we'll be welcomed with open arms, so my vote is for the Emerald Isle,' I say.

'The people of the Emerald Isle might be more welcoming, but they gossip far too much, so I was going to suggest the Outer Isles,' Rahfi says.

'I don't mind. They both sound fun,' Pippin says.

Aria gets the casting vote. 'Tricky. We'll have a sea voyage from either. It might be easier to find a boat from the Emerald Isle, but there are way more people, and as Rahfi says, they do like to chat, so word of our journey is more likely to get back to Sir Waldred. Overall, I think we're better off in the Outer Isles.'

'Right. So, the Outer Isles it is. Now, how do we persuade the portal to take us to that particular heart?' Rahfi asks, jabbing the symbol with his finger.

'Spin round three times on the heart and make a wish?' Pippin suggests.

'Too simple. There's no way that will work,' I scoff.

Rahfi shrugs. 'Probably, but no harm trying? It might work, after all, it didn't seem to be particularly complicated to get out of the cavern.' He walks up to the heart, spins three times and vanishes with a pop. Then a minute later he reappears. He opens his hand and holds out a prickly, purple flower: a thistle.

'You make it look so easy,' Pippin says.

'Years of meditation. I just focus on the destination and blocked everything else out. Anyway, at least we now know it works. Let's go through one after another. See you there!' A second later, Rahfi's gone.

Pippin skips over to the heart. 'My turn. Here goes. One, two, three …'

Nothing. She's still standing in front of us.

'Did you imagine the destination?'

'Course I did.'

'Try again. Picture it as clearly as you can. Feel the wind and taste the salty air ...'

Pippin closes her eyes and screws up her face. Her outline shimmers and she starts to fade. It's working! I hold my breath. Any minute now she'll vanish through the portal ... But she doesn't. Her image solidifies again. 'I thought you had it then,' I say.

She reopens her eyes. 'I thought I did too. I felt all wobbly, like jelly, but then nothing happened. It's not fair. Rahfi made it look so easy. I give up. You try.'

'You can try again later. Do you want to go next, Aria?' I ask.

'You go. I'll follow in a minute.'

She pushes me onto the heart. 'OK. If you're sure.' I squeeze my eyes tight shut and visualise the other heart, on a windswept island. 'Here goes ...' My eyes ping open. Around my feet, the sea sloshes in and out of a rocky pool. Just as well we didn't try this at high tide. The rock pool I'm standing in is unmistakably heart shaped. Nearby, I spot Rahfi kneeling beside another rock pool.

'Hey, Finn. You made it. Look at these ...' Wide-eyed, he points at a group of tiny translucent crabs in the bottom of the pool. The crabs roll their wobbly eyes, laughing at Rahfi. I explain he's from the mountains and never seen the sea, or a beach, and definitely not a crab before.

Rahfi puts his fingers into the water.

'Go on, I dare you,' one of the crabs says to his friend.

The crab runs up Rahfi's finger, out of the water and up his arm. Rahfi jumps in shock, slips, and lands in a heap in the rock pool. The crabs curl up on the bottom of the pool, rolling around with laughter.

A slightly bedraggled Rahfi settles back on top of a rock. 'I swear it did that on purpose,' he says.

I try not to snigger, but then a cloud falls over me. 'Rahfi, something must have happened. Aria and Pippin should be here by now. I have to go back for them.' I kneel down and whisper to the crabs, 'Could you look after my friend? If I'm not back before the tide comes in, make sure he doesn't get stranded on these rocks. I'd rather he didn't drown.'

'Can we play with him? Maybe an army assault up his left leg? Or we could nibble on his toes?'

'I don't think he'd like those games very much. Maybe you could just show him some cool stuff? A starfish? A sea-horse?'

The crabs sigh, but immediately start to plan the afternoon's entertainment options.

I return to the portal, squeeze my eyes shut again, and visualise the library. It turns out that opening the portal is much easier when you can picture the destination, and I'm back in the monastery in a flash. As soon as I open my eyes, I spot Aria sitting on the floor, hugging Pippin. I sink to my knees.

'What happened? Could you not get through the portal?'

She shakes her head. 'I didn't try. Pippin had another go, but she couldn't get it to work properly.'

I have an idea. 'Pippin, why don't we try together? Hold my hand.'

Pippin stands up and takes my hand. Together, we spin round. I visualise the rock pool and feel my body get light. Pippin's grip slips. With my free hand, I grab her arm. 'Don't worry, I'm not going without you.' Again, we start to spin, but again, I feel her slip through my fingers.

'It's not working,' Pippin says. 'I can't do it.'

Aria locks eyes with me. 'I'm going to stay here with Pippin. She's too little to leave on her own. You can go to the castle with Rahfi and deliver the relic for me.' She holds out the cube containing the feather.

I push it away. 'No, it's your relic.'

'Please, take it. Go on without me. We'll be fine here with the true monks until spring. Hobnob will look after us too, he's got a pretty good radar for spotting trouble. The elders won't care who brings them the relic, but we can't fail. You and Rahfi must take it to them. Please. If you don't, then it's all been for nothing. You have to go on without me.

I don't mind. I'll be able to go to the library every day. Maybe I can find out how to free Morgan.' Still protesting, she thrusts the relic into my hands and starts to spin me round. 'It's OK,' she says with a smile. 'Let yourself go.' Her eyes implore me to leave.

As I feel my body dissolve, I force my voice to shape the words, 'I'll be back as soon as I can.' I can't tell if the sounds were lost in the murk.

TWENTY-ONE

ELDERS

Next thing, I'm back in the Outer Isles. Head thumping and unable to see straight, my legs wobble and I topple into a heap. This teleportation malarkey is no fun. Rahfi helps me sit up. 'Pippin can't make the shift and Aria won't leave her. She wants us to go to the castle without her. First off, we need a boat. I wonder where the harbour is …'

Rahfi scans the coastline. 'Fifty-fifty chance of going the wrong way.'

'I'm going to bet it's that way.'

'Are you just guessing?'

'Educated guess. See how the trees are angled? The predominant wind must come from over there. So, if it was up to me, I'd put the harbour behind that headland, where there's more shelter from the wind. Nobody likes to anchor on a lee shore.'

'A what?'

'A lee shore. The one where the wind mostly blows in a direction that pushes you onto the shore. Much safer to risk being dragged out to sea by strong winds, than shipwrecked on the shore.'

Keeping my fingers tightly crossed, we start walking towards the headland. Several hours march later, we come to the crest of the hill. Beyond it, lies a small harbour. Sheltered by the headland, a number of fishing boats bob up and down at anchor. I breathe a sigh of relief. I was beginning to wonder if I'd made the wrong call and we should have gone the other way.

Rahfi shakes his head. 'Don't celebrate yet, that was the easy bit. Now we've got to persuade them to help us.'

We jog down the hill and onto the quay. I approach the nearest group of fishermen. They glare at me, their faces cut from granite, as unfriendly as their reputation. I open my mouth to speak, picking my words carefully, as polite as possible. 'Would any of you fine fishermen be available to make a trip to the Island of Gylen? My friend here and I would very much welcome passage.'

One of them pushes forward and stands in front of me, arms crossed. 'Mainlanders. We don't take kindly to your type in these parts. Take take take. That's all you ever do. You never give anything.'

'I'm not a mainlander, I—'

The ringleader pushes me roughly out of the way. I stumble backwards, landing on my bottom. The group laugh and walk away. 'Wait,' I cry, but they don't even glance back.

Rahfi holds his hand out and pulls me to my feet. 'Come on, there are plenty other boats here. They might be nicer.'

We walk the length of the quay with no luck. At the far end, we plonk ourselves down on a low stone wall. I bury my head in my hands. A stocky woman wearing a thick navy woollen sweater and oilskin trousers held up by string approaches me. 'Dinnae mind them, laddie, I'll take you. It'll be a nice wee outing. When were you wanting to go?'

'Thanks. Would now be convenient?'

The fisherwoman bursts out laughing, her face crinkling into deep lines. 'Now? Has nobody told you patience is a virtue? Best get busy then. Where's yer crew?'

I point at Rahfi. 'It's just us.'

She laughs. 'Nae worries. You look like fine young seamen to me.' She leads the way over to a small boat piled high with brightly coloured fishing nets. She pushes a bundle aside to make space for us. 'Sorry aboot the mess. I was daeing a wee bit of mending. So many holes in them there nets that the fishes swim right through. Hop on.' As soon as we're aboard, she lets the lines go and hoists an old sail with so many repairs it looks like a patchwork quilt. I breathe a sigh of relief, we're on our way to Castle Gylen. I wait for her to start asking questions about our journey, but she doesn't, chatting instead about this and that; the weather, the wind, the other fishermen. Her eyes fill with tears as she tells us her daughter moved to the mainland and now refuses to visit.

The Outer Isles are clustered close together, and it's not long before I recognise the craggy outcrops that make up the Island of Gylen. The fisherwoman brings the boat in towards the shore. The shallow draught means we're able to get a lot closer than with *The Alcina*. The island looks different. How long is it since we were last here? Ten months? Maybe more? In place of the barren and windswept land I remember, where only a few hunched trees clung to the rocky slopes, now, long golden grasses sway in the breeze and soft green moss runs down towards the beach. Are we in the right place? Yes, the unmistakeable ruins of Castle Gylen stand high on the cliff top.

'I'll just wait for you o'er there, looks a good spot to catch some mackerel,' the fisherwoman says. 'Holler when youse is ready to go.'

Rahfi and I set off up the path towards the castle. A few tiny blue and yellow flowers dot the hillside. Those weren't there before either: it's as if the island has sprung back to life. As we approach the castle, I spot the heavy iron portcullis blocking the entrance. How could I have forgotten about that? Last time we were here, a Guardian was with us, but this time we're alone. I check the gate for levers, although I know that the whole point of a portcullis is to keep people out, so putting a lever on the outside doesn't seem very likely. I'm not surprised to find nothing. Wildly jumping up and down in front of the portcullis, waving the relic in the air, doesn't work either.

'What on earth are you doing?' Rahfi asks, bemused.

I slump to the ground. 'I thought maybe the elders would be watching and see we'd brought them the relic. Then they'd open the door.'

'How did you get in last time?' Rahfi asks. 'Can't you just do the same again?'

I shake my head and explain how the Guardian chanted to make the portcullis open before.

'What if I chanted something?' he asks.

I shrug. 'Might as well.'

Rahfi starts to chant. Nothing. He changes the tune. Nothing. Again. And again. Eventually, he joins me, leaning back against the castle wall, and stares out at the sea.

'It's late. Let's go back to the fisherwoman. She must be wondering what's taking us so long. We're going to have to tell Aria we failed.' As we get up to go, Rahfi turns back to the portcullis and frowns. He starts to hum. The tune sounds vaguely familiar. 'What's that?' I ask.

'A nursery rhyme my mama used to sing to me, before she left me at the monastery. I don't remember the words, I'm afraid.'

'I recognise it,' I say. 'Keep humming.' After a few minutes, a faint voice joins him, then another, and another. The choir. 'It's working,' I cry, as the portcullis creaks and starts to inch its way upwards. When it reaches head height, we dart under. The voices stop and it slams behind us. Rahfi grips my arm. 'Don't worry. It did this last time,' I say.

I push the wooden door open and we step into the vast stone hall. The elders are seated around the table. My eyes scan the backs of the chairs, relieved to see several screens flicker with movement as they monitor Sea-Tamers all over the world. The other chairs are solid, wooden, carvings: their screens still frozen in time. If we have brought them the genuine

Air-Rider relic, then in the next few minutes we can free their clan magic and more screens will spring into life.

Kallan, my birth father and a Sea-Tamer elder, and the kind bird-like elder, who we now know is called Lady Philippa, push their chairs back and rush over to us. The others stand and give small, formal, bows. Only the thin elder who had demanded I take my place at the table remains seated. He leans back, folds his arms, and scowls at me. Clearly, he hasn't forgiven me for disobeying him. 'Where is Aria? Why did she not make the journey?' he snaps.

I explain about the portal, and how Pippin couldn't work it. At Pippin's name, one of the elders eyes flare, but they say nothing.

'Did Aria entrust you with the relic?' Lady Philippa asks.

I nod.

She takes my hand, leading me over to the centre of the room where a beam of sunlight pours through a window, landing in a golden pool on the stone floor. I hesitate before offering her the Air-Rider relic. It doesn't feel right for me to be handing it over rather than Aria. Yet I know I must. I take a deep breath and hold the cube out, the feather nestled on its silken bed. She holds her hands out flat and I place the cube on her palms. 'Thank you,' she says, placing the cube on the ground in the middle of the golden pool. She lifts the sparkling feather out and holds it between her fingertips. It casts a silver shadow on the ground that ripples with the movement of the relic.

Her voice floats through the air, 'There is no doubt you have found the Air-Rider relic. For this we thank you.' She summons two other elders over to join her. Together, they touch the relic with one fingertip each and it floats up above their heads. Silver light shoots out in all directions and the air crackles and fizzes. Images on the Air-Rider screens spring into life – another fragment of magic has been restored.

Then the feather sinks down to earth, drifting this way and that in the breeze. As it comes to rest on the floor, it's no longer made of glass. It's just a plain white feather. 'If it's OK with you, and you don't need it anymore, could I take it back for my sister? I think she'd like it, since she couldn't deliver it herself. She has a dreamcatcher and could knot it into the design to keep it safe.'

Lady Philippa nods. 'That would be fine. It has served its purpose.'

The thin elder grunts. 'Two relics are found, but those were the easy ones. What hope do we have of finding the next?'

TWENTY-TWO

QUEST

Kallan stands up. 'Don't be such a pessimist. Besides, we should not discuss these matters while we have a guest, we are not being good hosts.'

It hits me, if Rahfi isn't the Earth-Wanderer, I've made a terrible mistake bringing him here, after all, the location of the Council of Elders has been kept secret for centuries. Thanks to my thoughtless act of bringing a stranger, unannounced, uninvited, they might have to relocate. Another reason for the thin elder to hate me. 'I'm s-sorry,' I stammer.

All this time, Rahfi has been standing quietly to one side, his head bowed. Better late than never, I introduce him, 'This is my friend, Rahfi. He's training to be a monk, but he's been helping us. I think—'

'Step forward, boy,' the thin elder barks, his voice so sharp you could cut glass with it. Rahfi hesitates, then shuffles forward. The thin elder grabs him by the chin and twists his head from side to side. 'Elders, does this child remind you of anyone?'

The elders huddle together and start to talk in low voices. I can only catch fragments of the conversation.

'Can we trust ...'

'... protected from evil.'

'... powerful forces ...'

'... test ...'

'... only a child.'

The thin elder narrows his eyes, he knows I'm eavesdropping. 'Rahfi, who are your parents?'

'I don't know. They left me at the monastery when I was only a baby.'

The elders return to the huddle. Rahfi looks at me and shrugs.

Kallan breaks free from the huddle and stands in front of Rahfi. 'The likeness is undeniable. If you are who we think, then this is indeed a miracle.'

The thin elder draws himself to his full height, a good head and shoulders taller than the others. 'I knew your parents, boy. They were the last Earth-Wanderers to resist Sir Waldred's reign. They were the last thread that bound all the clans together. Until the day they were caught by his trackers, they sat here with us at this very table.'

Rahfi dips his head as if in prayer. 'I'm afraid that cannot be. My parents were no lords.'

'Indeed, they were ordinary folk, but status from birth does not earn a seat at this table. There are far more important values such as honesty, trust, fairness, respect, responsibility, and courage. Those values filled their hearts and souls. Before their capture, their work held the whole world in balance for, as long as an Earth-Wanderer sat at this table, there was hope. It is our belief that, by placing you in a monastery, your parents protected you from the rot that spread unchecked through the Earth-Wanderers under Sir Waldred's rule.'

I nudge Rahfi. 'See, I told you there would have been a good reason why they left you at the monastery. They didn't abandon you. They saved you.'

The thin elder ignores my interruption. 'It is clear the blood that runs deep is drawing the Relic Hunters together from the four corners of the world. With your help, the Earth-Wanderer clan may still be returned to a path of kindness. Yet, of all the Relic Hunters, you face the most dangerous quest. In fact, I fear it is impossible. For we know exactly where this relic is: it is held by Sir Waldred, and he has bound it to himself with ties stronger than any rope known to this world.'

'Please, let us try. We'll work out a way. I have no fear,' Rahfi says.

An elder with blazing red hair bangs his fist on the table. 'This is not the right order of things. We must free the Fire-Dancer clan before the Relic Hunters risk their lives on this death-bound quest.'

Kallan turns to him. 'But that is no easy task either. The Fire-Dancer is missing. You know the rumours. If Sir Waldred ...' He doesn't finish the sentence, but the implication is clear. The Fire-Dancer is dead. Which means the clan magic is lost. Kallan starts again. 'Without the child, looking for the Fire-Dancer relic is a fool's quest. A needle in a haystack. A puzzle without a solution. Yet here, drawn together by the deep blood, the Earth-Wanderer stands before us, ready and willing to seek his relic. Chance has presented us with an opportunity. We cannot let it slip through our fingers.'

Around the table, heads slowly start to nod.

'Great,' Rahfi says. 'Let's go and find Sir Waldred. Can't think of anything I'd rather do ...'

'That's settled then,' Kallan says, and the elders start to fade.

'Wait!' I cry. 'Don't go. There's another thing I need to tell you.' By now, the elders are no more than a shimmer. I'm losing them ... 'Morgan. It's about Morgan ...'

In a flash, Kallan's body solidifies again. 'What about my wife?'

'We saw her. We found out what happened to her. Sir Waldred gave her body to a demon called Algol. That's why she's gone bad. It's not her fault. We have to save her.'

One by one, the other elders re-materialise. One of them grips my shoulders and stares into my eyes. 'Algol? Tell me this is untrue. She was banished beyond the stars.'

The thin elder turns pale. 'I fear we have made a grave mistake. When the clans went into hiding, we cancelled the gathering. But she was still bound to that spell. She would have come back for it, but there hasn't been one in centuries. Indeed, I fear it is not only possible that she is still on earth, it's entirely probable.'

'She *is* on earth,' I insist. 'We saw her. And, thanks to Sir Waldred, she's in Morgan's body.'

'It is a grave thing, to cast a soul loose in order to have a body. There must be a gathering.' He turns to me, 'This is why you must take your seat at the table. You are needed. Every seat must be filled for the gathering. We must reunite the clans.'

I want to object, but I know that one day I must fulfil my destiny and join them. I take a deep breath, 'I swear I will take my seat, but there must be another way to save Morgan.'

A tight-lipped smile crosses the thin elder's face. 'There is only one other way to separate a demon from a human body, with a sword made from the rib of one of the frost dragons of Nikklheim.'

I gasp. 'But dragons haven't been seen in centuries. And Nikklheim doesn't exist, it's a mythical place.' Why would the elder set me an impossible task? I thought he wanted me to take my place at the elders' table.

'That is only partly correct. The dragons may be gone, but Nikklheim exists.'

'Where is it?'

'It is a sky-island.'

With that, the elders fade to nothing. Alone in the great hall, my voice echoes, 'Time to go.'

Rahfi scratches his head. 'Those elders sure do expect a lot of us, don't they? Find an extinct frost-dragon on a mythical sky-island and persuade it to donate one of its ribs to turn into a sword instead of eating us. Then bring them two more relics, one of which they have lost completely, and the other Sir Waldred has, so is almost certainly going to result in our deaths. And just in case, by some miracle we're still alive after all that, could we defeat a demon they forgot had been roaming the earth for a few centuries. No problem at all. Do you think we could have supper first, though?'

MOST DEFINITELY NOT

THE END

... NOT YET ...

DEAR READER,

Thanks so much for taking the time to read *Wild Sky*. I hope you enjoyed reading it as much as I did writing it. I'd love to hear what you think is going to happen next.

When I go to events, people ask me lots of questions. I thought I'd share a few here with you, but if you have more, please do send them to me.

Do you have a favourite character?

Most of them are based on people I know, so I love them all (except Sir Waldred of course), but I'll let you into a secret, Pippin's scenes are great fun to write. She has a mind of her own and often doesn't do what I'd planned for her!

Who are you most like?

Definitely Aria. We share a love of books obviously, but also, I hope I'm as kind and caring as she is. She is quite a bit braver than me though!

Are the locations real?

Many of them are, but I also made a few up, based on places I've been to. Castle Gylen is a ruined castle on a little island called Kerrera near Oban in Scotland. Spitbank Fort is one of a series of forts in the Solent near Portsmouth.

Where do you write?

I always write outside. *Eternal Seas* and much of *Wild Sky* were written on a boat, but I also like to write in the park and at the beach. My dream would be to have a beach hut so I could write every day, even when it's raining.

Reviews

If you enjoyed this book, please tell your friends! It would be great if you could also leave a review wherever you buy books online. Reviews help other readers choose their next book.

As well as online bookstores, there are many fabulous bookish websites, like LoveReading (www.lovereading4kids.co.uk), Goodreads (www.goodreads.com), and Toppsta (www.toppsta.com), where you can leave reviews.

Ask a grown up to help if you aren't sure how.

Thanks very much, and happy reading!

Lexi

Acknowledgements

Thanks to every reader of *Eternal Seas*, the first book in the Relic Hunters series, those who sent me messages and pictures, and all those who kindly left reviews. I absolutely love hearing about your favourite characters and scenes, and I'm delighted you found the adventure so exciting. I hope you enjoy the sequel as much.

Congratulations to the young illustrators whose amazing artwork is featured in *Wild Sky*. Everyone who entered the competition is incredibly talented and I hope you all carry on drawing. It was really hard to choose, but the winning artists are: Emily Aaban-Voss, Georgie Bryan, Lucy MacMahon, Stephanos Desta, Chloe, Yaqoob, and Yazeed. I was overwhelmed by the volume and quality of the artwork, and I'm delighted to share illustrations from the runners-up on my website: Robert Nwanze, Auraluz Parmintuan, Sophia Facon, and Guilia Minghella.

And a special mention to Charlotte Ward (11) who has designed bookmarks for the series. I hope we'll see more from all these young artists in the future.

I'm very lucky to have an amazing group of beta readers: Odinn Cockayne, Fritz Daly, Amelie and Sophia Fensome, Theo, Rafael, Lucy and Gabriel Harper, Amelia Leonard, Chloë Osborne, Marissa Salter, and Jack Turnbull. What a dedicated and professional team you are. Your input was so helpful and I hope you enjoyed seeing the book publishing process from the inside.

Another thanks to Odinn for naming the fire charm: kasai, which comes from the Japanese word for fire. And to Gabriel for naming the cat, Hobnob, after my favourite chocolate biscuit.

I have to mention Sarah Anderson for her input into the scene where Aria reads the stars. Sarah is the author of the *Starstruck* series, and is currently at university in Marseille, where she's studying Physics and aiming for a career in Astrophysics. She spends a lot of time hanging around in observatories and I drew heavily on her experiences. As with the sailing scenes, it was important to me that this was an accurate representation and, since I'm no expert in astronomy, her guidance was invaluable. As far as I know, she has never broken a telescope.

Of course, big thanks to Finlay, my son, for the constant support and encouragement, countless hours discussing the story, and the insistence on adding a rooftop chase. And to my husband for understanding when I disappeared into my editing cave, and for all the happy years of sailing we've had together, despite the occasional storm.

I couldn't have done this without my fantastic editors; Eleanor Hawken and Emma Mitchell. I look forward to working with you both again.

Author buddies, your encouragement, advice, and support has been invaluable through the emotional roller-coaster of publishing. There are too many to mention you all, but you know who you are.

Many thanks to the amazing and dedicated book blogger community. Not only have I been honoured to be featured on many of your blogs, but I have discovered so many other fantastic books through you that I will never see the bottom of my "to be read" pile.

Finally, I'm a member of several fantastic book clubs and organisations. I know not everyone can get to a physical book group, but I would happily recommend two on Facebook: The Fiction Cafe and The Book Club. I'm also lucky to be a member of several wonderful and supportive writer groups; Chindi Authors, the Society of Children's Book Writers and Illustrators, and the Society of Authors.

Thanks again,

Lexi

About the Author

Lexi Rees grew up in the north of Scotland but now splits her time between London and West Sussex. She still goes back to Scotland regularly though.

Usually seen clutching a mug of coffee and covered in straw and glitter, she spends as much time as possible sailing, horse riding, and crafting.

As with her other books, much of *Wild Sky* was written on a boat. Concentrating on not falling off makes writing tricky while horse riding. It is not recommended.

Resources

Lexi Rees runs a free #KidsClub designed to encourage a love of reading and writing for six to eleven-year-olds. Every month, subscribers get creative writing activities, giveaways, competitions, exclusive author interviews, book recommendations and other cool stuff.

You can join the club here https://lexirees.co.uk/kidsclub/

Get in touch

If you have any questions, you can contact Lexi via the website (www.lexirees.co.uk) or social media.

Happy reading!

Lexi